ANTHROPOSOPHICAL
FANTASIES

VOLUME ONE

[sic erat scriptum]

A Streetcar Named Karma

And twelve other stories

by Roberto Fox

Anthroposophical Fantasies

Volume One

Cover and other artwork by Celina MacKern

This book is a work of fiction. Names, characters, places, and incidents either are products of the author's imagination or are used fictitiously. Any resemblance to actual persons, living or dead, events, or locales is entirely coincidental.

by
Roberto Fox
Visit my website at
https://SouthernCrossReview.org/

Printed in the United States of America

Paperback edition:
ISBN-13: 978-1-948302-10-4
ISBN-10:   1-948302-10-1

Kindle edition:
ISBN-13: 978-1-948302-11-1
ISBN-10:   1-948302-11-X

Contents

A Streetcar Named Karma

Prague

A lecture wasn't exactly what I had in mind for the evening, but there we were, Katarina and I, approaching the hall where it was to take place. A full moon shone into the narrow cobblestoned street. Its presence more or less guaranteed that there would be no more snow that night.

That same day, I think it was early afternoon, I had boarded a streetcar and found a spot among the standees, when the clasp on my briefcase somehow opened as we rounded a sharp curve and the books and papers tumbled out. I bent to retrieve them and fell against another standee, knocking her over and falling almost on top of her. I stammered apologies in German, my native tongue, instead of Czech. My reaction was automatic, but the fact is that in that enlightened age all educated people in Prague spoke German. Hers was lightly accented. She helped me pick up my things, which were strewn around and soiled by the slush the passengers' shoes had tracked into the car. An elderly couple vacated a double seat at the next stop, and I quickly grasped the handguard and invited her to sit next to the window. I took my place next to her on the aisle.

She wasn't a beautiful woman, at least not in the usual sense. You could have called her attractive though. Her most salient feature was her smile, wide and spontaneous, lighting up her face. Though she wore a heavy fur coat against the cold, I could tell that she was somewhat plump, which was to my taste. And she didn't have the thin, bloodless lips of most German women; rather the full, sensuous ones of the Czech.

The bump, the fall and the shared retrieval task had served as an icebreaker, so I introduced myself and we talked and laughed about it and, naturally, I invited her to join me in one of those delightful Prague cafés for coffee and cake. But she pleaded a previous engagement, so I asked her to go with me to the theater that evening. She blushed, smiled, and said yes. When we reached her stop, she started to get off, but at the door she turned and said, quickly, "No, don't buy the tickets, but we'll meet there anyway. I'll explain later." The doors opened, and she stepped down and out. I noticed some of my fellow passengers smirking, but I didn't care about that, I was already in love — at first sight, as they say. A little boy sitting on the aisle stared at me with a fey look. I looked at him inquiringly and he turned away.

*

Katarina was already waiting at the theater entrance when I arrived five minutes early. She smiled, and I shivered more with expectation than from the cold. "I'm so sorry," she said, "but I forgot an engagement for this evening when I told you I could go to the theater." My heart sank, but she continued before I could say anything. "I'm going there alone though. Why don't you join me?" That was more like it. I agreed of course. "We must hurry," she said. "We don't want to be late."

"Of course not," I assented, although I couldn't have cared less. "Where are we going?"

"To a lecture, it's not far from here."

My heart sank again or, more accurately, took a little dip, for my idea had been the theater, then dinner with enough good German (or even Czech) wine. We were together though and that, although the circumstances were different from those I had anticipated, was sufficient to make me happy. She took my arm as we walked carefully over the icy streets.

A poster was stuck on the door of the lecture room. It said something about "Spiritual Science". My God, I thought, what have I gotten into? Many believe that now, the beginning of the twenty-first century, is a materialistic age. The fact is, however, that the first quarter of the previous century was at the apogee of materialism. Everyone believed in natural science then, and its findings and its arrogance were unquestioned.

The lecturer was to be a Dr. Rudolf Steiner.

The room, not very large, was almost full and there were no two seats together. Katarina sat on the aisle, and I had to sit two rows behind and to the right of her. This arrangement was unsatisfactory of course, but I appeased myself with the thought that I could at least observe her profile instead of Dr. Steiner's potbelly.

Exactly at the starting time he entered from a side door and stood alongside the podium instead of behind it. "*Sehr geehrte Damen und Herren ...*" A formal opening in a deeply resonant, Austrian accented voice. I had decided to listen with at least half an ear in case she wanted to discuss what he said afterwards, but that was impossible. Rudolf Steiner captured one's attention totally. He didn't have a potbelly, by the way. He was thin, of average height for those days, dark complexioned with pitch-black, straight hair. He was dressed

3

in black as well, except for a white shirt, with a frock coat and an artist's black silk tie. After the formal opening he became warmer, then, after a half-hour, very warm. He turned the world upside-down, saying things that were completely new to me, but which I somehow recognized as being true, as though I had always known them and was now being reminded. He spoke of a spiritual world that was real, of the nature of man as a spiritual being who is in a constant process of development through many lives.

My head swam, and I completely forgot Katarina's profile. In fact, at one point near the end I felt I was going to faint, so profound an effect did he and his words have on me. (Katarina told me later that people actually did faint sometimes, which could be embarrassing if they were sitting on an aisle. When this happened, Steiner didn't even pause while the unconscious body was dragged out into the fresh air.)

After it was over, and the thunderous applause died out, I sat alone. Katarina came and took my hand. I stood up and followed her out of the hall. I suppose the cold air brought me to my senses. We went to a café after all and I asked her about what had just happened, which was the turning point in my life, what was left of it.

We were together on the following two evenings, and never again. I was a lieutenant in the German army and had to leave on the third day for the front. It was 1914, and I, fool that I was, had volunteered to fight for our glorious fatherland. We spent our last evening together as lovers. I had an intuition that I would never see her again and I think she had the same feeling. Not that I believed I'd be killed in the war; young men never think that until it happens.

Sojourn

My sojourn in the other world was so brief because my life on earth had been so brief. It is only recently that I have had the ability to see my past life, parts of it at least, and to catch glimpses of the immediate future. I know that Katarina is here, because she also died young, and we will meet on a streetcar again. I've concentrated to the limit of my powers but have not succeeded in determining where I should look. Perhaps I shouldn't look, just wait for it to happen of itself like last time. But no, things have changed, and I must use my intelligence and will — and hope for luck, that's still allowed.

San Francisco

Luck came my way today. I switched on the TV and saw a picture of one of those famous San Francisco cable cars. Of course. Why hadn't I thought of that before? I flew to San Francisco and have been riding the cable cars for the past week. After the first two days I decided to ride only during rush hours — eight to nine in the morning and five to six in the afternoon — when there are standees and I can be one. A problem is that there are no curves to cause the accident. It has occurred to me that I could be in the wrong place. Once I was in Lisbon and rode on a similar streetcar, but with curves. It's probably still there. Lisbon doesn't change. But my intuition tells me he's in America and San Francisco seems to be the most likely place. No, "he" isn't a slip of the tongue. I haven't mentioned yet that I'm a woman in this incarnation and Katarina is a man; should be at least, it's the rule.

Today it happened. During the middle of the short uphill trip a handsome young man in an air force officer's uniform got on. I noticed that one clasp of his attaché-case was open, and I waited for the other one to spring. He placed the case

5

on the floor alongside his leg and opened a newspaper to read. The headline read: *U.S. Ground Forces Invade Iraq.* I decided to give karma a kick-off and nudged his attaché-case with my foot. It fell over and the other clasp clicked open. He leaned down and quickly picked up the case by its handle. The contents, loose papers and two books, flew out. Just as he bent down to retrieve them the streetcar's brakes squealed, he fell against me and we both went down, me on the bottom. He helped me up, apologizing and trying frantically to gather up his things. I looked out of the window to see what had caused the sudden stop. The driver leaned out and yelled at a little girl to watch where she was going, or she'd get killed. She looked at me from the sidewalk with that familiar fey look. Then she disappeared into the crowd. I helped him pick up his things and we sat in the seats vacated by a gay couple. After introductions and some small talk, he asked me to have dinner with him tonight. Naturally I accepted.

We are in a restaurant in Chinatown. He sips a glass of California wine and tells me that he's an instructor at a nearby airbase, but he's had no combat experience so he's requesting a transfer to the Middle East. It will be good for his career. He is so happy about it, so convinced, so foolish. Oh God, must it be a three-night stand again? Is there no way out? If I tell him what I know about us would it help, or will he think me mad? Behind him, on the wall, is a large mirror in which I can see the back of his head, myself and the street through the window behind me. My heart jumps when I see the little girl with the fey look outside on the street staring at me in the mirror. "No!" I cry and put my hand over my mouth. The little girl's fey look slowly relents, and she smiles.

"Is something wrong?" he asks.

I look into his concerned eyes and say, "No, everything's fine," because I know, I pray, that it will be different this time. When I look back into the mirror I see only the back of his head, myself and the window behind me. The little girl is gone.

by Roberto Fox

Life on Mars

Man needs but little earth for enjoyment, and still less for his final repose.

Goethe

"There **IS** life on Mars!" Gene insisted.

"I don't understand how you can make such an unfounded statement," Jerry countered. Jerry considered himself an intellectual, having completed two years of community college before he had to go to work for a living selling fifty cents a week life insurance to poor families.

"Yeah, that's bullshit," Bill Bunions agreed. "Not even Woody Allen believes it." His name wasn't really Bunions, but he was always complaining about them. Jerry and Bill were friends and almost always agreed on everything. Or, more accurately, Bill always agreed with Jerry.

I said nothing, chalked up my cue stick and lined up the Q-ball with the eight-ball, feeling somewhat behind it when Gene took my silence as, if not agreement, at least acquiescence to the possibility that there might indeed be life on Mars. He was mistaken. I merely considered the argument of much less importance than the possibility of winning ten bucks if I made my next shot.

Gene mentally zeroed in on me. I think he was already

planning to miss his own shot purposely — he was by far the best player among us — in order to be able to say, "Good shot, Frank," when the eight-ball teetered on the brink and finally dropped into the pocket with a clunk only a poolroom can acousticate. Eugene missed an easy one and I pocketed the ten. Speaking of pockets, "Pocket's" proprietor was Joe Pocket. An alias? — right. Joe had Sicily written all over his pockmarked face and "Pocket's" was probably the only authentic poolroom left in Brooklyn: no bowling alley, TV or video games (concentration was respected), and you paid by the hour to play.

After Jerry and Bill left and I was getting my coat, Gene invited me for a beer at the bar. I should have invited him, all of them in fact, as the winner, but I needed the ten bucks for a sandwich and carfare up to Columbia where I was a lab instructor. I wasn't really underpaid; my financial condition was due to an unhealthy taste for gambling.

Pocket's draft beer flowed through pipes that hadn't been cleaned since prohibition and tasted of rust, but we quaffed them down like men with a thirst. After offering to buy me another, which I graciously refused, Gene asked me to go home with him, he had something extremely important to show me. I told him I couldn't, that I had classes that afternoon, which was true, so he insisted that I drop by his place on my way home. I wasn't very keen on it because I figured he wanted to show me pictures of UFOs or something like that, but he was practically pleading, and what can you say to a guy who just threw a game of pool and bought you a beer to boot?

**

I rang his bell shortly after nine that night, hoping that

whatever he had up his sleeve would be short, so I'd have time to get home and change before meeting one of the other instructors. She was in anthropology, and I wanted to discuss the sexual practices of various primitive societies with her before getting to our own. Experience has taught me that the mere discussion of sex with women can make them hot, especially when you let them do most of the talking.

Gene didn't even bother to ask who I was through the speaker, just pressed the door-opening button and was waiting for me on his third-floor landing, first with a silly grin, then, as though remembering the seriousness of the moment, a sympathetic frown like a funeral home director's.

She was looking out the window when I entered the apartment and turned to greet me with a brilliant smile. She reminded me of Leslie Caron, the chameleon of "An American in Paris" (If you haven't seen it you haven't lived; get the video!) — petite, not exactly beautiful, but most attractive, or perhaps appealing is a better word — a *gamine* who might break out into ballet or the Charleston at any moment. She wore a light blue dress which matched her eyes; her hair was cut boyishly short. She was charming, I was charmed. I took the hand she offered and wanted to hug her, protect her, love her. Sex with her would not be hot and steamy, but more like diving into a cool, limpid lake. (I didn't think that then, only later — in fact it just occurred to me.)

"This is Nuria, Frank," Gene said. "uh, Nuria, this is Frank."

"I'm very pleased to meet a friend of Eugene's," she said. I was struck by two things. First, I wasn't exactly Gene's friend. We were neighbors, sometimes shot pool together, and I had been in his apartment (not an impressive place, by the way, although it was now at least clean) once before for a poker game. Second was that she spoke with an accent. The Leslie Caron resemblance suggested French, but her accent wasn't French. I couldn't place it. There was a third thought as well. If I had been so taken with Nuria just looking at her, Gene, the poor bastard, must be head over heels in love with her. I say "poor bastard" because I didn't think he had much of a chance. He had a beer-belly par excellence, a hanging jaw and he still had pimples, although he was at least thirty.

"And I'm pleased to meet you, Nuria. Ah, where are you from?"

"She's from Mars," Gene said matter-of-factly.

I dropped her hand and turned to Gene. He looked dead serious, but I had to laugh. "You mean the planet ... Mars."

"Yes, of course, and it's no laughing matter."

I turned back to Nuria, who was looking up at me with her almond-shaped eyes and a smallish smile. Gene must have gone bonkers if he was insisting in the poolroom that there was life on Mars because he really believed this girl, this Nuria, was a Martian. I could hardly take it seriously though. "Do you go along with that, Nuria," I said, smiling back at her, "that you are a Martian?"

"I do," she answered, and it sounded like a marriage vow. My heart skipped an octave as I wondered if these people could possibly be serious. Gene was the kind of oaf who believed in UFOs and ESP and drank carrot juice for breakfast, which didn't seem to do his complexion much good. He'd believe anything he wanted to. But the girl looked intelligent and, well, honest. The problem with honesty is that it's usually mated with innocence, which isn't a practical quality for our times.

I decided to try another tack. "But we've been to Mars, you know that little gadget roamed around taking pictures and there's nothing there — except the possibility that there was once water."

"But you see, Frankie ..." Why did she call me Frankie? Only my mother still called me that. "... we cover up the planet with a thin layer of virtual crust to fool you. And we captured the last two probes you sent up. Remember?" She patted my hand, and I tingled. "Please don't feel bad about it. We're afraid of your weapons and wars."

"Afraid of *us*?" I interrupted. "If you can do those things, you could probably blast us out of the sky."

"Oh, we wouldn't want to do that," she said sweetly. "We believe in peaceful coexistence. Besides, there are some things about you that we like. That's why I'm here."

"I see. And what are they, I mean the things you like?"

"I'm only at liberty to tell someone who is in a position to help us with them. Are you in that position?"

"If you mean do I have power or influence, I'm afraid not." I was aware that I was acting, talking at least, as though Nuria really was from Mars. Frankly, she was very hard to disbelieve.

"Do you know anyone like that?" she asked.

"You mean you want me to take you to our leader?"

"This is serious, Frank," Gene said, frowning at me. But Nuria didn't get the irony. "Yes," she said.

I looked at her and then at Gene and inspiration struck. "Gene, didn't you say once that Saul Bellow is your cousin?"

"Second cousin."

"Whatever. He's an important person."

"He's a writer, not many people read his books."

"He's a fucking Nobel prize winning writer, schmuck. Not many people read his stuff because it's too deep for them, that's all. He's got influence, man. All he'd have to do is call the President and —"

"He probably doesn't even know I exist," Gene said. "I only met him once at Yehuda Goldbaum's bar mitzvah."

"Who's Yahuda Goldbaum?"

"Another cousin."

"You see? he's nuts about cousins, even wrote a novella about them. Didn't he go to your bar mitzvah?"

"Nah, my old man didn't think he was a serious enough Jew, likes Rudolf Steiner and all," Gene insisted.

"So what? Lots of Jews like Rudolf Steiner."

"Not my old man. Besides, Bellow probably wouldn't believe us anyway."

"It wouldn't hurt us to find out. I mean if he's an anthroposophist" — that's what Steiner people are called - "he should have an open mind, especially about cosmetic stuff — I mean stuff involving the cosmos, of which Mars is a part."

Actually, I was kind of interested in Rudolf Steiner's Anthroposophy myself. One of his books fell into my hands — something anthroposophists would call karma — and I went to a meeting of the Brooklyn branch of the Anthroposophical Society where someone told me that Saul Bellow was a member — but in Chicago. And now Gene was saying he wouldn't believe "us", when I was still around because I was so attracted to Nuria. If she hadn't been there, I'd have been long gone. He had a point though, so I needed another inspiration. "Where's your phone'" I asked.

I called Shorty Jameson, another Columbia lab assistant, who was working on his doctorate and was sort of a genius in genetics. "Shorty," I said, "what would the genetic makeup of someone from another planet look like?"

"*Some*one?"

"Yeah, I mean it's a hypothetical question, for the moment, but just supposing that there was life on another planet, I mean advanced life, like humans."

"Who knows? What is this — a joke?"

Shorty didn't have much sense of humor, and he was easy to kid, which made him wary, so I had to convince him that I was serious. We grew up together in a pretty tough neighborhood and were the only members of our gang who got out of the rut and were educated. I loaned him the first book he ever read — *The Adventures of Huckleberry Finn* — which put him on the road up, so he owed me, as it were.

"No, this is serious, believe me, Shorty. Let's say someone from Mars or someplace came to Earth. Would they have the same genetic make-up as us?"

"Don't see how they could," Shorty answered after a pause while he was probably wondering whether he should answer at all. "They wouldn't have come from our genetic ancestors. Why are you asking me this nutty stuff, Frank?"

"OK, I know it sounds nutty, but if I were to bring you a

sample of a skin scrape or whatever it is you use, could you tell me if it came from a human being ... one from Earth that is?"

"Of course."

"And could you tell if it *didn't* come from Earth?"

"What's the difference?"

"Good point. How do you get the skin to analyze?"

"We have a special instrument for that, but you could use any sharp knife ... are you kidding me, Frank?"

"No, I swear to God, Shorty. Where's the best place to take it from?"

"What?"

"The *skin*, dammit."

"If you want to take a skin sample to analyze the DNA, you better bring the subject here." He paused while my mind raced. "It's expensive, by the way."

"Oh, how much?"

"A few thousand."

I found out later he was just testing me to see if I was serious. I knew he could do it for nothing when no one was around in the lab, at night, for example, when the rest of the geneticist nerds — including his boss — weren't around. Like now. Shorty was still working at ten o'clock at night. But he needed motivation for that. And I thought I knew how to provide it.

"No problem, Shorty," I said. "Wait there, I'll be right over." I hung up before he had a chance to protest.

It worked out just like I planned. We grabbed a cab and went to Columbia. When I introduced Nuria to Shorty and she swore that she was from Mars, he melted like an ice cream cone in Yankee Stadium in July. He led her into an examination room in order to take the skin sample and when they came out fifteen minutes later it was obvious he would have jumped off the Empire State building if she wanted him to.

***

It took a week for the results to be known. I asked Nuria where she was staying, and she smiled angelically. "Eugene has offered to put me up."

Eugene, Jesus! I didn't consider that good news but couldn't offer anything better because I was still living with Beatrice then, and she wasn't the type to welcome another woman into the "relationship", as she called it. So I needed another inspiration. You may have noticed that I'm pretty good at them.

"Well, I better stay with you," I said, stuttering like a schoolboy on his first date. "I mean like you're ... er ... like valuable and we wouldn't want anything to happen to you. Right Gene?"

"What's gonna happen to her here?" Gene protested as any red-blooded American boy would. "Besides, there's no room for —"

"Oh, that's a *won*derful idea," Nuria interrupted. "Then we can all be together."

That, needless to say, was the end of the "relationship". Nuria slept in Gene's bed during that week, and he and I slept on the living room floor like watchdogs — watching each other. We both took a week off work, I claimed that my mother was ill and I had to put her in a home in Florida. I don't know what excuse Gene gave. This was done without either of us telling the other, so neither had any advantage. The three of us took walks together in Central Park, went to the movies — Nuria preferred the old classics: West Side Story, High Noon, stuff like that, which weren't so easy to find, but in New York you can find anything within reason. Unfortunately, An American in Paris wasn't playing anywhere. She also liked to eat in MacDonald's.

***

On Monday morning the doorbell rang, and Shorty came bursting in with a huge envelope in his hands. "It's true, goddamit, she's not human! I mean she's human but not from Earth … you know … not an Earthling". He was panting from the run up the stairs.

Until that moment I had been putting on an act of sorts. I didn't really believe the Mars story but was so enamored of Nuria that I never admitted it. Now all that changed. "You mean you can prove that, Shorty?" I asked.

"Of course I can, it's all here," he said, patting the envelope. "Her DNA's just not ours, not even close to an Earth organism. It's incredible."

So, we had another convert. I looked at Nuria, who was sitting on the sofa sipping a coke. She smiled a smile that would have melted Darth Vader's heart. "OK, Gene, it's time to call your cousin Bellow."

"Well, I don't know …"

"Cut the shit and call him. We got evidence now. He could get us an appointment with the President."

"Of the United States?"

"No, of the fucking Girl Scouts. C'mon man, get off your ass."

Gene had to call a dozen cousins before he finally got Bellow's unlisted number.

"Call him Cousin Saul, Gene;" I said.

"Everyone calls him Sauly."

"OK, Cousin Sauly. He can't resist a cousin. He lives in Boston now. Tell him we'll be there this afternoon, that it's urgent, earth-shaking — but you better not mention Mars, yet."

"What if he asks what it's about?"

"Tell him you can't talk about it on the phone."

Gene had to name his mother, father, three aunts and a half a dozen cousins before Saul Bellow remembered who he was. "No, Cousin Sauly, it's not about a manuscript. I don't write," Gene said, sputtering into the phone. "It's really important ... er ... earth-shaking! ... no, I can't talk about it on the phone." Then *he* had an inspiration—finally: "It's about this really beautiful girl I'm with, I mean she's so special, you've *got* to meet her, Cousin Sauly, you just *got* to!"

That got him. Bellow was in his eighties and had been married five times and obviously couldn't resist a beautiful woman, the younger the better. America's greatest living writer, our cultural icon, but I'm the only one I know who reads him.

We took a cab to La Guardia airport and boarded the shuttle to Boston. Gene, Shorty and I pooled our money to buy Nuria's ticket. We were all nervous — frantic would be nearer to the truth, except Nuria, sitting between Gene and me, who calmly ordered a Coke, gulped it down and popped some chewing gum, which she loved. It was a beautiful autumn day without a cloud, and we could see New York on take-off and the sparkling eastern seaboard below us during the whole flight. Just touching Nuria's shoulder with mine occasionally or looking at her bare knees — she also loved miniskirts — was an infinitely better view as far as I was concerned.

***

Saul Bellow was expecting two people and didn't look very pleased to see the four of us. After giving us a once-over, his hooded eyes hardly ever left Nuria. We were in his study — three walls lined with books and the fourth a picture window framed by original paintings. Vivaldi's "Four Season's" purred forth from an invisible source. I was humbled being in his presence but also excited by the knowledge that we were about to deliver a cultural uppercut that even he could never have imagined. How was I to know at that point that it would be below the belt?

Gene started trying to explain why we were there, but he was so nervous he looked like he was going to faint, so I took over. I told Bellow that both Shorty and I were scientists at Columbia U. and were honored to show him the results of Nuria's DNA tests. Well, it took about an hour of explaining, cajoling, questions and answers, but it was mostly Nuria herself, her calm, simple insistence that she was indeed a Martian, that broke him down. Bellow sighed, poured himself a scotch and water, and nodded. Yes, he could arrange a meeting with the President.

He leaned towards Nuria, breathing heavily. "But what, exactly, is it that you want from us?" he asked.

Nuria's eyes dilated and turned yellow. She gazed deeply into the probing eyes of this man who was sixty years her senior — or centuries younger. Finally, she said it: "Disney World."

"What!"

"Yes, you see, we have heard so much about it and seen telepictures of it and our people are so curious and excited about it. We thought that if Mr. Disney could come to Mars for a while and show us how to make one ..."

"A franchise?" Bellow croaked. "For Disney World?"

He looked very angry and turned to us, probably thinking we were pulling his leg. But when he saw us staring at Nuria with dropped jaws, he groaned.

"So, you come as an emissary from Mars, you want to see our leader, and what you want from him is Disney World. Is that correct?"

"Yes, Mr. Bellow," Nuria purred.

He sank forward and held his head in his hands.

"Mr. Bellow, are you all right?" Nuria asked.

"Go on," Bellow muttered.

"What, Sir?" I said.

"Go on, get the fuck out of here, all of you," Saul Bellow growled without raising his head.

Shorty and I jumped, Nuria looked puzzled. Gene took her arm and walked her quickly to the door. She stopped before we could open it, turned to look at Bellow, who seemed to be sobbing, and said: "Goodbye, Mr. Bellow, I hope you feel better real soon."

"Poor man," Nuria said once we were outside.

The rest of us were in shock and didn't say anything as we shuffled aimlessly along a Boston street in the damp New England air. Suddenly Gene stopped and snapped his fingers. "Hey," he exclaimed, "how about trying Larry King? I think he's my cousin too."

"Oh good," Nuria agreed. "The king is just the person I want to meet."

Gene patiently explained to her that Larry wasn't *the* king, that we didn't have one, but that he conducted a popular TV interview show.

"Do you mean that I'll be on *tele*vision?"

"Well," Gene said, "it's entirely possible."

"Wonderful," Nuria gushed and kissed him on his pimply cheek. "They can see me on Mars."

*

EPILOGUE

After finishing this account, I sent it by e-mail to a friend with a scientific background for his opinion. Obviously under the impression that I had made it all up, he didn't say anything about the DNA part, but sent the following remark about Nuria's name:

"Nuria: I do not like the name. It simply sounds too Arabic. Remember Queen Nur of Jordan. So, I thought a strange but not non-existent name like Nysa would be better." (She was one of the nymphs who reared Dyonisius.

And Rudolf Steiner's nickname for Ita Wegman)

There was no use trying to convince him that it was true, especially because on Mars all women are called Nuria (and men Nurio). This has nothing to do with Arabic — or Spanish — culture, rather a coincidence. Only Shorty is disguised. He has been accused of falsifying the DNA test and has moved to another state. You may be interested to know that Nuria is now working as a tourist guide in Disney World . Yes, it has occurred to me that she may still be a Martian agent, but that doesn't worry me. What they want from us we could easily do without. She married Gene, by the way, despite his pimples, mostly because he was willing to relocate to Orlando, something which, despite my love for her, would have been too great a sacrifice.

The Purloined Poem

Geschichten schreiben ist eine Art sich das Vergangene vom Halse zu schaffen.

Goethe

I never asked my friend, Peter Product, the origin of his family name. I just assumed that it was shortened from one of those long, unpronounceable Polish or Czech names. In any case it raised eyebrows and, often, grins. Pete was a poet, a profession not very amenable to earning money, so he moonlighted as an assistant insurance underwriter at Encore Underwriters, Inc., 66 Wall Street, New York City, which is where I met him.

One day he hit the poetic jackpot when he wrote an epic poem with the title "Ode to the Brooklyn Bridge", dedicated lovingly to María, and had it published in *The New Yorker*. Getting something published in that magazine was enough to win Brooklyn's 3B (Best Breast-Beating) Gold Medal, so Peter Product's reputation went into orbit. Simon and Schuster approached him directly (he had no agent yet) for a book of his poems. S & S knew that they would gain no profit, but publishing poetry is good for a publishing house's reputation. Pete had a pen-drive full of his life's work, none of which, by the way, approached the poetic quality and heartfelt metaphoric feeling of "Ode". He sent it all to S & S, who edited it as best they could and issued it with the title *Ode to the Brooklyn Bridge — and other verses* by Peter Product.

In the real world, not even a successful poet can live on the royalties from one book of poetry, so Pete kept his job at Encore, for a while. His girlfriend — María, a dark-haired Argentine beauty — worked as a secretary at Encore, actually *my* secretary. I was a licensed insurance underwriter, Peter Product was one of my assistants. My section was growing and making a lot of money. Most of the other sections used the secretary pool, but I had the most important places in the country to cover: New York City and Kentucky. The importance of NYC is obvious, but Kentucky? It's the whiskey, stupid. Whiskey distilleries were and probably still are great fire risks, and their contents valuable. So risky and so valuable that no insurance company would dare to cover them alone. That's where Encore Underwriters came in. We would distribute the risk over various companies, even including Lloyd's of London. The latter, the biggest insurance company in the world, would automatically accept fifty percent of any risk if our American companies combined would take the other fifty percent.

First, I'd hired Peter, then María, without knowing of their relationship. If I had known I certainly wouldn't have hired them both. The complication was that I fell for María, but she had already fallen for Pete. My situation was hopeless because company policy forbade intimate relationships between managers and underlings of the opposite sex, for example: male manager, female secretary. It was further complicated by the object of my affection's lover also being my underling. There was one advantage to this situation though. Although it would have been improper for me to be in an intimate relationship with María, it was harmless if I hung out with María and Pete together — although it was like inquisitional torture. When we sat together in a bar or in their apartment or walked in Battery Park and they cuddled and held hands I felt like I was being burned at the stake.

But allow me to get to the crux. After Peter Product's poem was published in *The New Yorker* and his book was published by Simon and Schuster, everything changed. Although young women generally prefer poets to clerks — if money isn't important that is — a successful poet is an irresistible target. They stick to him like ants to a honeypot. The result was that Pete neglected his work — and María. He began to hang out with the unwashed, bearded, pot-addled fellow poets in Greenwich Village. He even wanted to live there. And, María suspected, he was shagging a free-verse poetess from Brooklyn, whose muse's initials were LSD.

That's when María rebelled. She'd had enough of potheads in Buenos Aires who, despite having talent, mostly musical, were broke, stoned and rock crazy. Her appreciation of rock and roll ended with the Beatles. So, when Pete moved to a communal pad in Greenwich Village she left him. He claimed that he simply had to soak in the artistic atmosphere where his muse was more likely to visit his soul; she told him to go fuck himself with a broomstick. (Profanity always comes easier to non-native speakers who are not intimidated by its shock value.) I of course was more than willing to let her cry on my shoulder, playing the avuncular card, which wasn't hard. After all, I was fifteen years older than María, ten older than Pete.

I didn't actually fire Pete, just had a man-to-man talk with him one day after work in *Smokey Joe's Wall Street Irish Pub*.

I suggested that he would be happier devoting all his time to artistic creation than merely moonlighting at it. I even offered to loan him a thousand dollars to tide him over until the royalties from his book began to stream in. If you think that this was an indication that I was desperate to get rid of him, you'd be right. He stared at me for a few moments, took a big gulp of beer, and started to tear up. I didn't know what to make of that. Did he need his miserable salary to support an invalid mother I didn't know about? Had he been diagnosed with cancer and needed the company's medical insurance plan? But, no, it was nothing like that. On the contrary, he was overcome by emotion and gratitude. He said that he had been thinking of resigning, but didn't want to leave me in the lurch, as it were. He feared losing his second-best friend, after already losing his first, María. He grasped my hand, knocking over his beer glass, which luckily was almost empty. For a moment I was afraid he might kiss my hand.

Although Peter Product was tall and gangling, handsome in a way and probably well-endowed you know where, as such tall and gangling guys usually are, and I am short and almost bald and no poet, but solid I'll have you know. María finally saw the light and fell into my arms, outside of office hours of course. I warned her of the dangers inherent in boss-secretary office romances. At first, I worried that she'd back off, but she actually liked it. A secret affair is often more exciting as long as nothing goes wrong. Just in case though, the new assistant I hired was a sixty-year-old plumpish woman.

About six months later it happened. I almost didn't notice, but María brought my attention to the article in *The New York Review of Books*. A graduate student in English

Literature from Redbrick University, UK, unearthed a nineteenth century book of poetry containing an epic poem by C.D. Maypole, titled "Ode to the London Bridge". Except for the title and some thees and thous, it was an exact replica of Peter Product's Ode to the Brooklyn Bridge. At first the student thought that the author had used a nom de plume but soon tracked her down as having been baptized in 1789, died in 1822 in Reading, England. She found no other literary work by her. The student accused Pete of being a plagiarist, because he must have somehow also found that book and simply changed the English spelling and some archaic words.

"Wow!" I said when I finished reading it. "Poor Pete."

"Poor Pete my ass," María rejoined. "Poor *hijo de puta* is more like it." The news spread like wildfire, at least in literary circles and the office. There was much divided opinion: some pitied him, others damned him. But all agreed that he was a schmuck. His reputation was ruined, Simon & Schuster withdrew his book from circulation, and he was banished from the Greenwich Village communal pad. Poor Pete.

Several months went by before María and I received the same email from Peter asking us, practically begging us, to meet him the following Saturday at midnight at 333 Atlantic Avenue, apartment 5E, Brooklyn. What the hell! María and I exclaimed. I emailed him back for both of us, saying we could meet him right here at Smokey Joe's Wall Street Irish Pub. But he insisted that we go to Brooklyn, that what he had to tell us was so extremely urgent and delicate that it must be kept "Geheim", for now. María, who is quite a linguist, told me that *Geheim* means secret or occult in German. We decided to humor him; after all, he had been our colleague, my friend and María's special friend. I was also by now sufficiently certain that María was over him and at least comfortable with me.

We took a taxi to Brooklyn because I didn't want to leave my car without a bodyguard on a Brooklyn street at midnight. Apartment 5E means the fifth floor — without an elevator. When I rang the bell, Pete leaned out of a window near the roof and called out: "Is it you guys?" as though he didn't want to reveal our names. "Yeah, us guys," I yelled back. He buzzed and we began our journey up to 5E.

When we arrived, panting, Pete pulled us in and locked the door. It was one of those old downtown Brooklyn buildings where large apartments had been subdivided into smaller ones. The one we were in was large enough for a living-dining-bedroom-kitchen rolled into one; at least the bathroom was separate. Ms LSD was sitting on the sill of the window Pete had called us from. She was wearing only panties, no bra, although she didn't really need one. Actually, in order to avoid a false impression, she was quite pretty — short blond hair, full lips and great legs. She ignored us and stared out the window, ready to howl at the moon, should it appear.

"Thanks for coming, really thanks," Pete intoned. He embraced me and tried to do the same with María, but she backed away. "Can I offer you something?" he asked. We noticed the pile of dirty dishes in the sink, so we declined.

"Just tell us why we're here, Pete", María said "That's what you can offer, it's late."

"Oh sure," he said. "Here, let's sit here." We sat on rickety chairs around a scarred table, María and I on one side, Pete on the other. LSD didn't move from her windowsill.

"Okay," Pete began with a cheesy smile. He was nervous, tapping the fingers of his right hand on the table, noiselessly because he'd bitten his fingernails to the quick. "There's one thing I gotta tell you guys, and you must believe me." He looked from María to me and back. We didn't say anything or even nod, so he went on. "Do you remember that poem, *Ode to the Brooklyn Bridge*?" A rhetorical question so we didn't bother answering. "Well," he said, "I really wrote it and I never saw that book with *Ode to the London Bridge* in it, and I'd never heard of C. D. Maypole."

"Can you prove it?" María asked with acid in her voice.

"No ... not in the usual way." He began tapping with all ten fingers.

"Will you please stop banging on the table," María said.

"Oh, sorry." He withdrew both hands from the table and held them on his lap.

"What do mean by not in the usual way, Pete?" I asked him as gently as I could, although I felt like kicking him in the teeth. Why doesn't he finally admit that he purloined the poem for God's sake?

"Has either of you heard of Madame Blavatsky?" No reaction. "Or Rudolf Steiner?"

To my great surprise María said, "Blavatsky was a theosophist, Steiner an anthroposophist."

Pete seemed surprised as well. "Yes, yes, María. How do you know about them?"

"My crazy uncle was an anthroposophist, he talked a lot about it, and he had books, mostly in German, but some in English and even a few in Spanish."

"Crazy?" I said, hopefully.

She laughed; her attitude was changing. "He wasn't really crazy, but some people called him crazy, kidding, because he believed that stuff."

"Did you read any of those books, María?" Pete asked. "Do you believe it, too?"

"I read a couple, skimmed them really." She paused, looking at Pete in a different way, as if she knew what was coming. "I'd say I'm agnostic about it; I mean it's pretty weird stuff."

"Weird?" I said.

"Sí — and cool too."

"Yes, Yes, exactly," Pete gushed, "Cool!"

She was smiling and it disturbed me. I thought we'd come to hear Pete out — I admit that I'd been curious — but then to tell him very sorry, and don't bother us again.

"Listen Pete," I said, "if you got us here to listen to a lecture about Hinduism or something, we're not interested."

"No, Steiner wasn't a Hindu, he was an Austrian philosopher, and he westernized reincarnation, so to speak." He looked at María, who nodded. "That stuff, reincarnation and karma was Buddhist, Hindu, Indian stuff, but Steiner brought those ideas to the west and even combined them with Christianity."

"What does that have to do with your poem though — or *her* poem?" she asked.

"If you can believe that I really wrote my poem without having seen hers first ..."

"We didn't say we believe you," I interrupted.

"But just for a moment if you could accept it hypothetically, that what I say is true, what does it mean? A coincidence?"

"Hardly," I said. "Look Pete, I'm not calling you a liar, it's possible that your subconscious convinced you that you wrote that poem alone. Stuff like that happens."

"But then I'd have had to have access to *her* book first. Right?"

"Well, yes, but ..."

"I didn't, I swear it. So ..."

"Is your mother alive, Peter?" María asked him out of nowhere.

"My mother? Why no, she died when I was a boy, but why do you ask that?"

"Swear on your dead mother's memory that you are telling the truth."

Pete looked at her with bulging eyes. Then, as though completely beaten, he hung his head and murmured, "No, I couldn't do that, it would be ... dishonorable. She has nothing to do with this."

María jumped up from her seat, facing Pete, leaving me the only one still sitting. "OK," she said, "I believe you now, that you never saw the other poem, but how do you explain that yours is identical?"

"But María," I objected, "he won't swear on his dead mother's memory. How can you say you believe him?"

"In my country men are always swearing on their dead

mother's memory, and they're all fucking liars. Now I know that Peter is honest. Don't you see?"

"No."

"If he was lying, he would have sworn on his mother's memory."

"Why?" I said. "That doesn't make sense."

"He refuses to dishonor his mother's memory, which means he's honorable. Don't you understand?"

I didn't, but I let it go, because LSD had approached. I noticed now that her breasts, though small, had large rosy nipples. She stood facing me. I didn't stand up because I knew I'd be a foot shorter.

"I can explain it," Pete said. "There's only one explanation. You see, when Rose here" — he nodded at LSD — "introduced me to Rudolf Steiner, and I began to meditate on my past lives, I realized that I am the reincarnation of Claire Maypole, so ..."

"Claire?" María interrupted, glancing suspiciously at Rose, "Were did you get that name?"

"I found her, in my meditation that is. My middle name was Dorothy, or Dorothea, not so sure of that."

"Did you say *my* middle name?" I screamed. "You're stark raving fucking *mad.*"

Rose put her hand on my shoulder, to calm me down, I guess, and it worked. I felt as though I'd been touched by an angel, my heart slowed down and my neural functions as well, because what happened next is a blur. María and Pete went over to the window Rose had vacated and were talking and hugging; Rose was massaging my scalp and I fell asleep with an incipient erection.

Against my advice, but with María's blessing, Pete announced to The Village Voice that he was the reincarnation of C.D. Maypole and that's how he knew the words to *Ode to the Brooklyn Bridge*: he remembered them. It was just right for the Village Voice, so they printed an interview with Pete. Larry King read it and brought Pete for a live unrehearsed interview on CNN's Larry King Live. Nobody actually believed him, except for a few outcast anthroposophists, but Pete was so obviously sincere and enthusiastic that the story was picked up across the country, even worldwide. Pete's book was reissued, and he became famous and financially secure. So he had everything, even María. And I? Well, Rose gives a great massage, and she fits me better than María ever did. Why? Because she taught me what I was lacking: Anthroposophy, the name of Rudolf Steiner's spiritual science. That was her secret, luckily, not LSD.

by Roberto Fox

The Girl in the Floppy Hat

My infrequent trips to the States, on family business or just business, were almost always uneventful. But the last two had been the most eventful journeys of my life. The first began with a four-hour bus ride from my home in a remote corner of Argentina to the city of Cordoba, where I entered a travel agency a few minutes after three in the afternoon and approached Luciano's desk. He stood up, smiled automatically and held out his hand. As I took it his smile vanished as quickly as it had appeared and he said, "You traveling today ... or tomorrow?" and I knew something was wrong.

"Today, of course."

He looked at me, obviously puzzled, then shrugged. "Correct, no problem. For some reason I thought it was tomorrow."

Part of my work as a consultant to agricultural cooperatives is to analyze misunderstandings. Do you know what the problem is? People don't listen. Luciano sat down and clicked away at his computer. I sat across from him and glanced at the calendar on his desk: Friday, January 8. I was about to say "Hey, Luciano, you should keep your calendar up to date and you'd know when your clients were traveling," but instead I opened the newspaper I'd bought at a kiosk outside the agency just before entering and looked at the date: Friday, January 8. My face felt hot, and I was glad that Luciano was busy changing my reservation and couldn't notice my embarrassment. I had left home a day early. It made no difference for what I had to do in Florida, except that I wanted to leave on Saturday and arrive on Sunday morning in order to rest one day and get busy on Monday. Now I'd have a Saturday on my hands. Still, it was the first time something like that had happened to me. I might misplace my glasses now and then, but a whole day!

"Wait here just a minute, Sr. Frank. I'm going to the airline to change the ticket."

I went to a café on the next block and ordered a cafecito while I read the newspaper. It was mostly about the economic recession, unemployment and the political party infighting in Argentina and, naturally, the war in Kosovo. All depressing stuff, but more depressing, for me, was the reason for my trip to Florida — to transfer my mother from an Assisted Living Facility to a nursing home and get Medicaid to pay for it. I walked back to the travel agency and found Luciano at his desk listening to another passenger's woes. He handed me my ticket in a plastic envelope, and I inspected it carefully.

"All in order, Sr. Frank," Luciano assured me. "You still have plenty of time to get to the airport."

"Did you reserve a car for me?"

"Yes, of course, Interamericano. Have a good trip." He scuttled back to his client and peered into his monitor. "Hey, Julieta," he called to the girl at the next workstation, "what's the code for Santiago de Chile?"

"How should I know? Look it up."

"SCL," I said, smugly I fear, as I picked up my bag and strolled toward the door, and they all turned and looked at me.

The short flight to Buenos Aires was on time and uneventful. I passed an hour of the three-hour wait for the connecting flight re-reading Carson McCuller's "The Heart is a Lonely Hunter". I had chosen it because it's small and light — not in content but in weight. I bought some pipe tobacco in the tax-free shop and walked around the transit lounge observing my fellow passengers boarding in Buenos Aires as they drifted in. The usual mix of nervous tourists already dressed for Disney World and businesspeople looking like their next important meeting would be immediately after take-off. I saw the girl in the floppy hat shortly before the flight was called. Tall and very thin. Her hat covered the upper right side of her face. She wore an ankle-length blue skirt slit up to the back of her knees and a wrinkled cream linen jacket and heelless sandals. Bare feet aren't very sensible for air travel. I had to smile when I realized that I was worried about that. You often see under-dressed tourists who think that because their destination is warm it will also be warm at thirty-thousand feet and arrive sneezing. But why should I be worried? Maybe because she looked so fragile. The idea of approaching her and suggesting that she put on socks was ridiculous. I'd long since learned that unasked for advice is almost always unwelcome. Besides, where would she get them? I couldn't very well offer mine. The flight was called forty minutes before departure time, the usual procedure for getting hundreds of passengers into a 747 and still depart on time.

I put the book into my carry-on and stood up as they

called for passengers holding seats in rows 32 through 43 to board. The girl, who had been standing the whole time, suddenly sat down and pulled a pair of gray woolen socks from her overnight bag. She took off the sandals and slipped on the socks. I smiled and nodded in her direction: Atta girl.

I had an aisle seat so I wouldn't have to climb over people to go to the toilet or roam the aisles. A window is preferable if there's anything to see, but we were leaving at eleven at night and arriving at 6.30 in the morning. When I got to row 33, there she was in the window seat. I don't believe in coincidences, which doesn't mean that every time you sit next to someone on a bus or airplane it's part of your karma, but this time I had already been watching her in the terminal and worrying about her feet being cold. I mean what are the odds?

I said *Hola* as I placed my carry-on under the seat. She smiled and nodded as she took off the hat, rolled it up and stuffed it into the seat-pocket in front of her.

Jet black silky hair blended nicely with her green eyes. She turned and gazed out the window at the runway lights, which soon became star lights, and I opened *The Heart is a Lonely Hunter* and read the same paragraph three times before giving it up.

"Pollo o pasta?" the flight attendant mumbled with a lack of enthusiasm fully shared by the passengers. My ears were still stopped up so I didn't hear the first word and said, "Pasta o *qué*?" "Pollo," she repeated. "Pasta," I said with a shrug in my voice. My companion ordered the pollo and said to me, "It's chicken." I realized she thought I hadn't understood, being too obviously a gringo, so I said to her in Spanish, "Ah, you wanted to help me, but my ears were only stopped up."

She blushed and nodded. I ordered red wine and water and she water only. We ate in silence until I decided it was time to put a deeper crack in the ice.

"This pasta has no taste at all," I said. "How's the chicken?"

"It tastes like pasta."

We laughed. "But the wine doesn't taste like water," I said. "Like a drop?"

She held out her plastic cup. "Well, just a drop." I leaned across the empty seat and poured her several.

"Are you from Buenos Aires?" I asked her.

"No, Santiago de Chile. Do you know it?"

"Yes, I've been there often. Chilean women are the most beautiful in the world, or so I've been told."

"You've been told," she said with a wide-open smile. "And have you no opinion?"

"Oh yes, I agree entirely."

"Thank you, in the name of Chilean women ... and you're American."

"Is it so obvious?"

"I saw your passport," she admitted as she went at cutting the chicken with a plastic knife, "when you were in the tax-free shop."

That was even before I noticed her. So she's interested. Fancy that.

"Do you live in Florida?" she asked me.

"No, in Cordoba, not so far from Chile really. Do you know it?"

"Only from the air. It's on the Pampas, isn't it?"

"Part of it is, but I live in the mountainous part.

"Oh, that must be nice ..."

And so it went until they announced that the movie would be *You've got Mail*. "Do you have Internet?" I asked her.

She nodded. "I hear the movie is good, but I can barely keep my eyes open."

I leaned between my legs and fished in my overnight bag for a notebook and pen. "Let me take down your e-mail address and I'll give you mine." I moved into the middle seat, wrote my address on a page of the notebook, ripped it out and handed it to her, together with the notebook. "If we miss the movie, which seems likely, whoever sees it first can tell the other about it." Admittedly a weak excuse for moving closer to her and finding out her name. She read my name and e-mail address, hesitated a moment, then wrote her name and e-mail address in the notebook.

"You know, Mireya," I said, feeling pressed for time because her eyelids were already fluttering from the effort to stay open, "I might have the weekend free and go to the beach. Maybe you'd like to come with me."

She looked into my eyes as though asking who I was and what she should answer. I should have been surprised but wasn't when she said she'd like that. "I'm staying with friends in Ft. Lauderdale," she said so softly that I had to lean over to hear. She wrote a telephone number in the notebook.

"Perhaps you can call me when you know."

"Yes, I will."

"What beach do you go to?" she asked. "I hope not Ft. Lauderdale or West Palm Beach. I don't like them."

I laughed. "Good, I don't either. I prefer Singer Island. Do you know it?"

"I've heard of it but have never been there."

"It's north of West Palm, and considerably cheaper."

She nodded and yawned as the movie flickered to life. We watched without sound for a while. Then her head sank slowly onto my shoulder, and I could smell her faint perfume. I closed my eyes and slept.

The flight is only seven and a half hours, so what with reaching cruising altitude, eating and the bumps and grinds of the plane, it's impossible to get more than a few hours' sleep. In my case even less, as I was careful not to disturb her head on my shoulder (remember the song?). In the morning, she looked wan and seemed even thinner as we walked together through the finger gate and separated at the immigration desks. I promised to call her on Friday afternoon and kissed her on the right cheek. Her green eyes seemed very large in that pale face as I turned away and breezed through the US citizens line while she waited with the lesser mortals.

*

It was a hectic week, which didn't give me time to face what I was doing until the last moment when I said goodbye to my mother — perhaps for the last time. She sat in a chair in the room she was to share with another nursing home resident. "Do you have to go already?" she asked. I didn't really, but I was exhausted from running from the Medicaid office to banks, my mother's Assisted Living Facility, real estate agents and nursing homes. And the fresh sea smell and Mireya's faint perfume was luring me away from the rancid odor of age. I walked quickly, almost ran, through the wheelchair traffic to the elevator, waited impatiently for its slow-motion doors to close and, once on street level, burst into the sunshine and across the parking lot. I flipped on the Honda's air conditioning to full and pulled away. I phoned Mireya from my motel and offered to pick her up in Ft. Lauderdale the next morning, Saturday, but she insisted on meeting me halfway, said a friend would drive her. So, I told her to go to Federal Highway and Glades Road in Boca Raton at nine o'clock, or earlier if she wanted. She said nine was fine. The rhyme woke me up to the fact that we were speaking English. She had about the same amount of accent in English as I have in Spanish. I had a quick supper in a Denny's, watched TV a while and went to bed early.

It was one of those beautiful sunny Florida mornings. I arrived at the corner in Boca Raton five minutes ahead of time and she was already there, standing alone dressed again in a long skirt, but of a lighter color and fabric than the one she wore on the plane. A plain blue polo shirt revealed that she was pretty flat-chested. And the same floppy hat. I had expected to see long tanned legs in shorts, which was what everyone else was wearing, including me. An overnight bag was at her feet though, which was definitely a good sign. My heart raced and I told it to slow down, that this was probably no more than a one-night stand.

I pulled up to the curb and leaned over to open the door. She got in, took off the hat and smiled her wide-open smile.

Her teeth were large and white and her mouth sensuous — to me at least — and somehow innocent at the same time.

"Hi," she said in English.

"Hi, were you waiting long?"

"No, about five minutes. I was early, I think."

"Yes, so was I."

She leaned over and kissed me on the cheek. I swear it burned. "That's for being early," she said, and looked front with her hands in her lap, smiling softly.

"It's true then," I said.

"What?"

"That it pays to be punctual."

We got onto *I 95* heading North. I was busy maneuvering us through the weekend traffic to our destination in one piece, so we didn't say much. The radio was tuned to NPR, where they were on a Gershwin kick. Mireya moved her lips to the songs and hummed a little. She had a sweet voice. She asked me to put the air conditioning down although it was already low. I don't care for it myself, but in Florida it's necessary. I turned onto Blue Heron Drive, crossed the bridge to Singer Island and pulled into a Days Inn I know there. Once in our large Florida-sized room, I asked her if she'd like to go for a swim before it got too hot.

"You go," she said. "I'd like to just rest a little." Rest? It was only ten o'clock.

I hadn't seen the ocean in months and wanted to now. Should I just change in front of her, or do it in the bathroom? She solved the problem by going in herself.

The water was pellucid and warm. I dived in, swam a few strokes and floated with my face in the sun. There's something strange about her, I thought. First of all, no young woman in her right mind would go off for the weekend these days with a total stranger who could turn into Juan the Ripper at the first glimpse of moonlight ... and the clothes ... long skirt while traveling when everyone else her age wears jeans or slacks or shorts ... and the floppy hat.

I rode in on a minuscule wave and walked back over the hot sand to the hotel. The wave of anticipation I felt wasn't entirely sexual; it was more like the confusion of emotions usually associated with an adolescent's first love. I shook my head to myself in wonder. I had brought a key with me — a keycard rather — so I let myself into the room, which was on the ground floor. The air conditioning had been turned off and only the blower was on, sucking filtered hot air into the room. She was lying on the bed naked with her legs spread and her eyes closed. Was I surprised, despite everything? You bet. She was even thinner than I had imagined, with nipples like brown buttons perched on petite breasts. Almost a boy's body; the muted feminine curves were there though. I closed and locked the door and crossed to the bathroom to shower trying, unsuccessfully, not to think while I did so. How old would she be? 25? Well, let's give her 27. What kind of performance was she expecting from a weary stud in the autumn of his discontent? I thought as I wiped off the steam and looked at myself in the mirror. Well, no time like the present to find out.

I lay down beside her on the bed half expecting her to twist around and lock me in a passionate embrace, or at least turn her head and smile, waiting for me to initiate the overtures. But she didn't move, and I realized from her breathing that she was fast asleep. What the hell do I do now? One of my greatest shortcomings is that when I don't know what to do, I usually do nothing. In this case, however, it turned out right. I closed my eyes and fell asleep, which was easy after the sea swim and the sun.

I woke with dark curtains of hair draped on both sides of my face and clear green eyes looking into mine. "How beautifully you sleep," she whispered. She moved on top of me and I barely felt her weight. "You will be gentle, won't you?" she asked. "I know you are a gentle person." I nodded as well as one can with his head on a pillow. Somehow words wouldn't come, not even "yes". I lifted my arms to embrace her.

"Please," she said, urgently it seemed, "don't touch my back."

Why not? What would happen if I touched her back? It reminded me of the Chinese princess who always wore a ribbon around her neck. When the prince secretly removed it while she was sleeping her head fell off. I let my arms fall outward like a man on a cross. She started to reach for my penis.

"Mireya, er, don't you think we should use some kind of protection?"

It took a moment for her to understand what I meant, long enough for my erection to sink and, I thought in mild panic, perhaps never to rise again.

"Oh, I don't want that, do you … really?"

"Well …"

"Are you afraid of AIDS?"

I'm deathly afraid of AIDS, yes. "No, but ... well ... nowadays ..." I felt worse than a coward, I felt like a traitor, an enemy of love.

"You don't have to worry," she said, smiling artlessly. "I haven't been with a man since my first boyfriend, and that was ten years ago." She put her face next to mine, relaxing. "The incubation period is less than that, isn't it?"

"Yes," I said, "but what about me? I mean you don't know me very well."

"I don't know you at all," she murmured in my ear. "Yet I know you perfectly, and for such a long time. I'm not afraid, really"

I didn't know what to say to that, so I just lay there in crucified mode.

"There is one thing though," Mireya said, lifting her head to look at me. "I cannot get pregnant."

"Of course not."

"So ... so maybe you're right. I mean that would be ..." she searched for a word — "unfair."

Unfair to whom? I thought, but said, "Don't worry." I was thinking that I'd pull out before ejaculation.

"Could you ... could you not come?" she asked. That was quite different, but I confidently agreed. And, wondrously, my erection agreed as well. I was gentle, very gentle, moving slowly or not at all. She arched over me, reached for the ceiling and moaned, then fell down and the black curtains covered my face. Soon she rose again, reached this time for the stars and seemed to attain them for her moan was more like a soft scream. After the third time I knew I couldn't hold out much longer, so I eased her off and we lay pressed together for a long time. She slept for a few minutes, and I felt pleasure at having given her such pleasure.

It was dark out when we got out of the bed. Neither of us had eaten anything since breakfast, and I didn't know if she had even had that. When we were washed and dressed, we went to the hotel's restaurant, ordered swordfish and white wine and I prepared myself to ask her some questions, but it wasn't necessary. She started talking.

"Did you wonder why I didn't want you to touch my back, Frank?"

"As a matter of fact, I did. I thought maybe it was some kind of reverse fetish."

She didn't laugh. "You see, I had an operation and there are some ugly scars on my back." Tears formed in her eyes, but she blinked several times rapidly and they were gone. Or maybe it was my imagination.

"What kind of operation?"

"I had lung cancer — or I still have it, I don't know."

That explained a lot, but I wasn't sure how. I took a healthy gulp of wine. "Tell me about it, Mireya."

"You can see them," she said quickly. "It's just that I didn't want you to today. Can you understand that — or is it too silly?"

"Yes, of course. Today's special."

She took my hand. "Yes, it is. Very special."

"It's all right, I don't need to see them," I said, and I honestly had no desire to.

She pushed back her hair. "I've had it for twelve years, not on the lungs, that started two years ago. It began on my leg. They cut it out and I took Anthroposophical medicine. Do you know what that is?" I shook my head. "It's something like homeopathy, but better. I'm sure it's what has kept me alive so long."

"And is it cured now?" I asked. I wanted it to be cured.

"I don't know. That's why I came here. There's a wonderful surgeon here, a friend of my family who operated on me the last time. I don't mean the leg," she added quickly, "I also had a lung operation." Then, barely pausing, she said, "I've really been very lucky. You have no idea how kind people have been to me." I wouldn't call having lung cancer exactly lucky, but I didn't say so.

"And other friends paid for my trip. You see, a few months ago they discovered — that was in Chile, where I have a wonderful doctor but he's not a surgeon — he discovered small nodules in each lung — just one in each."

"I see," I said. "And the last time, I mean the operation?"

"That was much worse. He took out almost half of both lungs." She frowned. "But sometimes even small things are serious."

"Yes."

"They haven't grown, but the doctor wanted to examine me anyway and take new x-rays and other tests."

"So that's what you were doing during the week?"

"Yes, that's what I was doing. And do you know what he said?" Suddenly she was like a happy child. "He said he didn't see the need for another operation, that they looked insignificant and if they don't grow, I should be all right."

I squeezed her hand and blinked myself this time. "That's wonderful, Mireya."

"Now do you see how lucky I am? Then I met you, which was the greatest luck of all." Our table was lit only by candlelight, so she didn't see me blush, but I must have looked puzzled and embarrassed, for she said, "Don't you know why?"

I shook my head, it's all I could do.

"Because I love you ... and you love me, I can feel it. Isn't it so?"

And then I cried, I actually cried real tears, silently, with my head down. It was the first time I had cried in many years. I'm not the emotional type. "Yes, Mireya, it's true that I love you, but I'm the lucky one for that, not you."

"Then we'll both be lucky," she said, smiling, and lifted my hand to her lips. "But you see now why I always wear these long skirts and that silly hat."

"I do?"

"I would love to wear shorts as they all do here and run along the sand and dive naked into the sea ... but I can't. I have to keep out of the sun and almost any strenuous activity tires me. I'm sorry, darling, it must be such a bore for you."

"Not at all," I assured her, "I can show off my muscles better this way. You just sit and watch."

"I have and you have beautiful muscles."

"Ah-ha, at last I've caught you in a lie."

"It's not a lie, it's true," she giggled. "They're just not very big."

"But beautiful."

"Exactly." She giggled again. "I'm not supposed to drink wine, either." She sipped and looked over her glass at me like a wanton sinner. "And if I got pregnant, I just don't know what I would do."

"Of course, I understand."

"You know, if I wasn't ... ill ... I'd never have come with you here." Her eyes glowed blue-green in the candlelight. "Time is against me though. Something has happened inside me that I can't contain, that I don't want to contain. Because I don't think I'll have the opportunity to feel something like this again."

She did tire easily. I had to almost carry her to our room, even help her undress. She was out like a light as soon as her head touched the pillow. I went down to the sea and looked at the stars a long time before joining her. The next morning, she stayed in bed. She said she was fine, just wanted to rest luxuriously, that she was spoiled. In the afternoon we went to the beach, and she sat in a rented beach-chair with an umbrella over it and watched me swim from under the rim of her floppy hat. During the drive back to Ft. Lauderdale we didn't say much. Her head was on my shoulder, and we were just there, together.

From then on, we communicated by e-mail. I have saved her side of the correspondence because it's so eloquent and moving. My side was ... well ... me. I went to Santiago a few times on business and stayed the weekends with Mireya. The last time she was in bed with what she called an attack of weakness. She had a small house in her parent's garden — a living room that doubled as bedroom, a kitchenette and bathroom, everything in miniature. I slept on the floor beside her narrow bed, a far cry from the room at the Hilton Carrera that my client was paying for, but infinitely more satisfying. She said she was going to her sister's place in the south of Chile for a few months and asked me to visit her there the week after Easter when her sister, Mónica, would be going to Santiago. But Mónica didn't want to leave her alone, so that would be our excuse for my being there. She described the mountainous area in glowing terms, adding that one day she wanted to live there forever. I said yes, of course I would go, that I couldn't wait. "Oh, that will be wonderful!" she cried and hugged me so hard that she began to cough and had to lay back again.

It was during that visit that she played a recording. A sweet voice singing *lieder*. "How do you like it?" she asked me with a mischievous smile. "She's very good," I said, and meant it. "She's not German though, is she?"

Mireya laughed. "No, I only memorized the words." My surprise was evident. "Yes, I studied singing at the conservatory and the teachers thought I had a brilliant career ahead of me. Naturally I can no longer sing." Her eyes were saying, Don't worry, I'm happy anyway.

Mireya had no access to Internet in the south of Chile, but I phoned her frequently. On the Monday after Easter Sunday, as I was about to leave for the airport, the "Wellness Director" at my mother's nursing home called from Florida to inform me that my mother had died in her sleep. It wasn't unexpected, in fact in a way I was glad because Mom had certainly had enough of being a child in an old woman's incontinent body. The conflict with my coming visit to Mireya was foremost in my mind. I hesitated, then said I would be in the nursing home early on ... no, the following day was impossible ... the day after, the third day after her death. I had just called Luciano to change my booking from Santiago to Miami and was about to call Mireya to tell her I'd be delayed when, on impulse, I decided to check my e-mail. There was one message waiting to be read. It was in Spanish from Santiago de Chile:

Estimado Don Frank,

Mireya died today, Easter Sunday. She had a brain tumor that grew very fast and wasn't diagnosed. She was thirty years old. She will be cremated today in Santiago.

With deep regret,

Mónica

*

I had selected an aisle seat as usual, but the flight was lightly booked so when I reached my row I sat in the middle seat, an old trick to avoid anyone sitting next to me and closed my eyes. I had just lost the two people I loved most in the world and didn't want some boozy shoe salesman feeling sociable sitting next to me. As we were rolling toward the runway, I felt someone climb over my knees and into the window seat. I sighed and was about to move to the aisle seat when someone sat in it as well. So much for solitude, I thought. Well, I'll ignore them. The aircraft shuddered as it strove for altitude, and I glanced to my right. Mireya, with the floppy hat still on, smiled softly and rested her head on my shoulder and I could smell her faint perfume. My skin tightened and my head felt as though it was burning. My first thought was that the telegram had been a mistake or a sadistic joke. I knew that wasn't true, but it was all I could imagine. I tried to say something to her, I forget what, probably just her name, but my lips and throat were parched, and nothing came out. So, I just sat there, more or less in suspended animation, when the person on my left put her hand — an old, liver-spotted hand — on mine and patted it three times, then folded her hands in her lap and looked forward. My mother had never liked flying and preferred to be as far from the window as possible.

I closed my eyes again and thought how fortunate I was to be accompanied by the two women whose love I was entirely unworthy of, at least for the next seven and a half hours.

by Roberto Fox

The Spell

Jenny Howard picked her way through the mud paths of the Brazilian *favela* until she found the hut she was looking for. Dona Josefina was sitting outside peeling potatoes with her legs spread apart so the peels would fall into her wide skirt. Jenny was an American school teacher under contract to an anthroposophical foundation dedicated to enhancing educational levels in the third world using Waldorf pedagogy, the system initiated by Rudolf Steiner in Germany almost a hundred years ago. An idealistic young woman, Jenny was prepared for the sacrifices inherent in that kind of work — but not for black magic directed against herself and her loved ones.

"Good morning, dona Josefina. I'm Jenny, from the school,"

"Good morning, my dear," dona Josefina said, quickly looking up without missing a beat of her peeling. "I am so glad you've come to see me. We are the two most important women in the favela and it is good that we finally know each other." Jenny was surprised to see a gentle smile on her lips. "Please sit down and tell me why you have come."

The day before Jenny had pushed open the unpainted, waist-high gate and walked into the front yard of her small, rented house. She paused a few feet from the door in order to extract the key from her bag. As her eyes moved down to the bag she saw something on the worn doormat that caused her to take a step back and place her hand over her mouth: a chicken's head with the blood not yet dry, alongside it two broken vials with their contents of red and yellow powder spilled out over the mat. Anyone who lived in Brazil would recognize a *Macumba* spell. Jenny breathed deeply several times, fished out her keys and stepped over the abomination.

Once inside, Jenny dropped her bag on the floor and sat down heavily in an overstuffed armchair. Her fingers were trembling, so she clasped her hands together. Who could hate her enough to do such a thing? Her brooding lasted only a few seconds though. She stood up quickly and took a plastic trash bag from a drawer in the kitchen. Outside she rolled up the mat with the chicken-head and powder inside it, put it in the bag and burned the whole mess in the backyard. She didn't want Divino, her foster child from the favela, to see it when he came home from school.

Then she phoned Pedro Branco, a sociology professor at the university of Sao Paulo and the man who wanted to marry her. "What really bothers me is that someone would want to harm me, even if they chose that ridiculous way to do it. I thought I was, well, at least well liked," she said.

"They love you, darling," Pedro assured her. "But you must have offended someone, probably without even realizing it".

Jenny gasped.

"What is it?" Pedro asked

"I was just thinking of who it might be."

"What are you going to do?"

"Do? Why nothing, of course."

"But what if ..."

"If it happens again, I'll complain to the police about someone putting trash on my doorstep."

The door opened and seven-year-old Divino ran in. Jenny smiled and waved to him. He ran up to her and she bent down to kiss him.

"Divino just came home, Pedro," Jenny said. "I just wanted to get it off my chest to someone who wouldn't be horrified. Gotta go now."

"Jenny."

"Yes?"

"Macumba isn't something you can just ignore."

"Oh, Pedro, really," she laughed. "Not you too, professor. Look, we'll talk about it on Saturday, okay?"

"Sure, but ..."

"You're full of surprises, darling. Maybe that's why I love you. Bye now."

After supper Jenny read a fairy tale to Divino and put him to bed. Then she prepared her classes for the next day and went to bed herself. Before sleeping she concentrated on a meditation recommended by Rudolf Steiner: a detailed retrospection of the day, from the end to the beginning. Despite being tired from her exhausting day, she slept fitfully. A heavy weight seemed to have descended on her heart, which annoyed rather than frightened her. She was not, she assured herself, afraid. She dozed off ...

"Yenny! Yenny!" It was Divino screaming.

"Divino!" She sprang out of bed and ran into his room. She switched on the light and saw him standing on his bed pressed up against the wall staring in horror at the floor. A Yayar 's flat, triangular head, red tongue flicking, was raised above its yellow-ringed body alongside Divino's bed.

"Don't move, Divino, don't scream, I'm here." She was able to control her panic only because of Divino's greater need to control his. She stamped on the wooden floor and the snake, the most poisonous in Brazil, dropped its head to the floor, turned it toward Jenny and raised it again. She stepped backwards into the hall, ran to the kitchen where she grabbed the ax she used for chopping wood for the fireplace, and rushed back to Divino's room. The Yarar ducked its head in a little bow and whipped its body around, so it was pointing at Jenny. They stared, each waiting for the other to move. Finally, the snake swished its tail and began to advance. When it was a yard away from her, Jenny swung the ax down with all her force. It struck just behind the Yarar 's head, chopping it off and burying itself in the floor.

Jenny ran to Divino who was standing like a statue on his bed with urine running down his leg. She hugged and kissed him, and they both fell onto the bed sobbing.

"Someone put that snake in Divino's room," Jenny told Pedro the next morning. "Or do you think the Macumba spell hexed it out of thin air?"

"No, someone must have put it there," he agreed, "but it's the spell that gave him the courage to do so."

"What do you mean?"

"Whoever it was feels that he's protected by the spirits once the spell is activated. It's a dangerous situation, Jenny."

"Yes, after last night I believe you," she admitted.

"Do you know who the local Macumba priestess is that the favela people go to for ... ah ... advice?" Pedro asked her.

She thought for a moment. "Yes, I think so. A dona Josefina, she lives in our favela."

"Go to her, Jenny."

"But Pedro, that's ridiculous."

"I know but go to her anyway."

"I will not give in to such superstitious nonsense," she insisted. "I'm a spiritual scientist, not a spiritist.

"That would be fine if only you were involved, but it looks like they're after Divino."

"Divino?"

"Of course. Do you feel that you have the right to risk his life?"

"But why?"

"Because it's the best way to get at you. Do you have any idea who might be behind it?"

"Well, no, not really."

"Do you want to sleep at my place tonight?"

"I don't know, I'll let you know. I have to go now."

*

"Do you know who could have cast the spell?" dona Josefina asked after Jenny had told her the story.

"I've thought about that, and I think that ... well, that it might be Zeca."

"The boy who works in the clinic?"

"Worked in the clinic. I had to let him go."

"Why?"

"We have a professional nurse now from America and Zeca was jealous, I suppose, and told the patients that she didn't know what she was doing."

"Ah."

"But worse, he said that she was working for the devil."

"I see," Josefina said, looking hard at Jenny. "And is she?"

"Of course not. She's extremely competent and knowledgeable and Zeca isn't. I warned him, but he kept it up. He was endangering our work, so I told him he'd have to leave."

"How did he take it?"

"He didn't say anything. Just left. It was very difficult. He's been with me from the beginning."

"And he's the only one?" Josefina asked, continuing to peel her potatoes.

"Yes, I'm sure there's no one else."

"I believe you. You are well loved here."

"Thank you."

Jenny waited for her to say something else, but she remained silent, peeling.

"What do you think I should do, dona Josefina?" Jenny finally asked.

"You should have come to me immediately, before

crossing the threshold into your house. There is white Macumba and black Macumba. You have become a victim of the black. You must understand that firing Zeca in favor of a foreign woman was a tremendous blow to his male Brazilian ego". She sighed and her bosom heaved. "But you cannot change your decision now, it would mean giving in to the spell. You must fight it. Come this evening to our meeting."

"Where?"

"Here. And bring the boy."

Jenny was reluctant to go to a Macumba ceremony, white or black, but she was even more reluctant to continue living with the spell hanging over her — and Divino, whom she loved more than anything or anyone else in the world.

As Jenny and Divino approached Josefina's shack that evening they heard wild drumming and smelled the penetrating odor of wine, incense and blood. Jenny hesitated at the door, but it was opened from inside and Sergio, one of her older pupils, solemnly took her hand and led them in.

The first thing she discerned in the semi-darkness was a black woman dressed entirely in red kneeling in a circle in the center of the overcrowded, candle-lit room. She held a convulsively twitching chicken fast while dona Josefina, in a tent-like white gown adorned with pearls and stars, knelt in front of her with a large knife in her right hand and a bowl in the left. One eye was half-closed and the other goggled fearfully. Her hair was unbraided and flowed loosely over her shoulders and face like a dark cloud.

Dona Josefina deftly slit the chicken's throat and caught its blood in the bowl. Then she poured in oil, wine and honey, dipped two fingers in it and slowly drew crosses on the other woman's forehead and throat.

The woman in red drank the horrible brew and immediately went into ecstatic convulsions similar to those of the slaughtered chicken, fell down, sprang into the air, danced wildly and finally threw herself onto the floor and rolled her eyes. Another woman went into the circle, knelt, another chicken was sacrificed and so on, some fifteen times in Jenny's presence.

At intervals the drums stopped beating, dona Josefina tinkled a little bell and all was still. She moaned something about *Domini* and suddenly the singing, dancing and twitching continued.

The room was crammed with sweating people, black and white, male and female, and many children who delightedly clapped their hands and sang along, as did Divino. Jenny wanted to draw the children around her as a protective wall.

Suddenly dona Josefina seemed to come out of her trance. She smiled and walked heavily to the door. They all poured out into the humid air. But it was only a break for costume change. Soon they were inside again for the second act.

The atmosphere was completely different now: calm and solemn. The initiates, *filhas de santos*, were dressed in blossom-white gowns trimmed with lace. They formed a circle around a white tablecloth spread on the floor. A child put candles and flowers on it, then six plates. A woman brought Bahia food. Six children were permitted to eat of it.

"It is an exorcism of the spirits who harm children," the woman next to Jenny whispered.

When the children finished, a seventh plate was placed

on the table and heaped with Bahia food. Josefina approached Jenny and Divino and held her hands out to them. Jenny expected the worst. The Bahia food was a concoction of manioca meal, a green liquid and a mountain of meat that would stick in her throat if she tried to eat it. But even worse was the cup being filled before her eyes: the chicken-blood cocktail.

It turned out that Divino was to eat the food and she drink from the cup. The boy picked up the dripping chunks of meat and chewed them heartily as Jenny stared at the cup and then at the solemn, sweating faces surrounding her. If she didn't drink it would be an unpardonable offense. This was, after all, a religious ceremony. And why was she there if not to exorcise the spirits — real or otherwise — that threatened to take Divino from her?

She took a deep breath, closed her eyes, picked up the cup and drained it, praying that she would not vomit it up.

Immediately the solemnity was transformed into violent drumming and dancing. Jenny thought she must faint, but somehow, she didn't, and she even managed to keep the onerous brew down.

Finally, it was over. Josefina kissed her and Divino and the others laughed and congratulated her. She walked out of the shack clutching Divino's hand, and they headed up the hill towards home in the starless night.

"Look, Yenny," Divino whispered, and pointed to the top of the hill.

Jenny looked and saw a gaunt figure in gray shorts silhouetted against the sky. It was Zeca. Jenny pushed Divino behind her and drew a deep breath.

"It's all over, Zeca," she called out.

Zeca remained standing there clenching and unclenching his fists.

"Go and don't come back or things will go badly for you," Jenny yelled and raised her own clenched fist. "Dona Josefina has exorcised your spell."

Zeca staggered backwards as though he had been struck. Then he turned and ran down the other side of the hill towards the avenida.

"The yayar won't come back tonight, will it, Yenny?" Divino asked. Jenny scooped the boy up and placed him on her shoulders.

"No, Divino, it's dead and will never come back again."

ANTHROPOSOPHICAL FANTASIES

by Roberto Fox

A Multicolored Goddess in Anthroposophical Heaven

by Roberto Fox as told to
Frank Thomas Smith

Chiche invited me to a lecture at the local Anthroposophical Society on Saturday evening. I had planned to go to the opera, where a traditional version of *The Magic Flute* was being presented at the Colón Opera. I have seen many versions of Mozart's masterpiece, my favorite, the most recent being "modern" (in quotes because I have come to equate modern with crappy where opera is concerned). The traditional version only attracts true Mozart lovers, so I knew that I would have no trouble obtaining a ticket for a later performance. Chiche is the nickname of one of my ex-clients who became a friend. I was able to discover the fate of her husband during the dictatorship through my contacts in the Federal Police. He had been drugged, weighted and thrown out of a helicopter into the Rio de la Plata — the updated Argentine method of New York mafia killings where boats were used to the same effect and the body is never found. It was one of the many reasons why I decamped from Argentina and sat out the "dirty war" in the U.S. I didn't want to be one of them. The information meant the end of hope for Chiche, who was already along in years then, and now she is in her eighties. She is a wonderful, courageous, intelligent woman, a school teacher by profession, and I didn't have the heart to refuse her invitation.

She is an anthroposophist, that is, a disciple of Rudolf Steiner, and this was not the first time she tried to get me into the fold. Although I find Steiner's writings interesting, even fascinating, I have no desire to become a true believer, which is, as far as I can see, what most members of the Anthroposophical Society are. Chiche told me on the phone that the lecturer was a young Uruguayan, especially invited by the Argentine society because a few members had heard him speak in Montevideo (Uruguay), and were convinced that he is an initiate a la Rudolf Steiner. Chiche was quite excited by the whole thing and said she wanted to know my opinion. I suspected, however, that her real motive was to broaden my interest in Anthroposophy by giving me the opportunity of listening to a real initiate.

The Society owns a small house in the suburbs of Buenos Aires, easily identifiable by an organic architectural façade designed according to anthroposophical insistence on no right angles. Inside the house is like any other, except that two rooms have been converted to one large one painted in pleasant pastel colors, where the lectures take place. The lecturer, Ramon, was not so young after all — although for Chiche everyone under seventy is young. He had developed a technique of walking back and forth while speaking without notes in his Uruguayan sing-song Spanish, using hypnotic arm movements. Although it was less than a year ago, I can't for the life of me remember anything he said. But that may not be as much a reflection on his words as the fact that my attention was directed elsewhere.

Two rows ahead of Chiche and me and to our right sat a striking woman. Not the least remarkable aspect of her anatomy was her flaming red hair, fastened at the back of her neck and from there flowing down her back like blood. Most people with red hair have fair, freckled skin, but hers was dark, either deeply tanned — unlikely at that time of year unless she went to one of those sun parlors — or the result of a favorable gene symphony inherited from a Brazilian or African grandparent. Her nose was aquiline and her lips (another contradiction) were full. She wore a cream-colored knee-length dress which adorned beautifully shaped crossed legs which seemed to be distracting Ramon in his travels, for he stopped most often in front of her when he wanted to emphasize a point. And why not? She was a multicolored goddess in anthroposophical heaven.

Afterwards came the worst part: tea and cake when cocktails would have been more to my taste. Normally it would be time to escape, but I hung around hoping for a chance to meet the goddess. And lo and behold here comes Chiche leading her to me.

"Roberto", she gushed, "I want you to meet Mireya. Mireya Calderón, this is Roberto Fox."

Following the local custom, I kissed Mireya on the right cheek. As I withdrew I noticed a faint line of pink fuzz on her upper lip, somewhat magnified by the heat in the room. I couldn't help wondering if her pubic hair was also red. I found out later that it is dark red, but that's getting ahead of myself.

"Mireya *Fernandez*, Chiche, remember?" Mireya said.

"Oh yes, sorry," Chiche said, shaking her head. "You know the latest feminist fad, Roberto, women using their maiden names instead of their husbands'. Nothing I can do about it I suppose."

"Legally, Chiche, my name is Mireya Isobel Fernandez de Calderón. The first three names are mine; the rest indicates that I belong to Calderón — which I certainly do not."

"Probably Rudolf Steiner would have approved," I said slyly.

Chiche laughed. "Touché. Anyway, Señora Hernandez, I wanted you to meet Roberto Fox, who's very good at finding things."

"Charmed," she said with a charming smile and a deep, for a woman, voice. "The pleasure is mine," I replied in all seriousness, "but I sometimes can't find the keys to my car, so I can't vouch for the validity of that recommendation, Chiche." She was about to say something when Ramon appeared at her side. "Oh, Ramon, a marvelous lecture, thank you so much."

"I suppose it was satisfactory, but I thank you for the opportunity to give it here," Ramon said, somewhat pompously I felt, but perhaps I felt that way because he was looking at Mireya from the corner of his eye. I know about these gurus, anthroposophical or otherwise: women flock to them like boys to soccer heroes. Mireya, though not as tall as I thought when I only saw her seated, was nevertheless taller than Ramon, and she peered down at him, as I did from my even greater height. Chiche introduced us, the obligatory kiss on Mireya's cheek followed and a handshake for me.

"Tell me, Ramon," Chiche said, "did Dr. Steiner ever say anything about flying saucers?"

"Certainly not," Ramon smirked. "That's hardly spiritual science," — with emphasis on the last word. Then to Mireya: "I hope you found my little talk interesting."

"Yes, I did, thank you very much for coming."

"It's my pleasure. Do you have any questions?" Translation: your place or mine?

"Many," Mireya said innocently, and I knew it was time to butt in.

"Why did you say 'certainly not' about flying saucers?" I asked him. "Even Karl Jung wrote a book about them."

"They're nonsense and Dr. Steiner had no time to talk about nonsense. Furthermore ..." An overweight lady intruded, happily, into our little circle. "That was a *wonderful* lecture, Señor Ramon. I have the impression you're an initiate. May I ask you something?"

Chiche leaned toward Mireya and me and whispered, "Come outside, you two. I want to speak with you — privately." At first I thought she was disappointed at Ramon's dismissal of the saucers, but it turned out to be otherwise. We went to a café on Avenida Cabildo, two blocks from the Anthroposophical Society, and ordered cheesecake, a specialty of the house, and coffee. I was thankful not to have eaten any anthro-cake. When I looked at Mireya, I was surprised to see that her hair no longer seemed red. Was it a wig? I didn't see her take it off. She noticed that I was staring and smiled. "Are you looking at my hair?" I nodded. "It's a very strange thing. When I'm in the Anthroposophical Society it's red, anywhere else and it's normal, this kind of undefined color. I suppose it has to do with the colors of the walls in the Society reflecting onto my hair."

Chiche put her hand over hers. "No, my dear, it's a sign that you belong there."

"What did you want to talk to us about, Chiche?" Mireya

asked, obviously wanting to change the subject and probably curious as well. I certainly was curious, especially if it had something to do with Mireya and me together. I hoped Chiche didn't intend to invite us to a flying saucer landing.

"Mireya," Chiche said, "I want you to tell Roberto all about Pablo's disappearance. Now don't look at me like that." Mireya didn't seem to be looking at her in any special way, so I assumed she meant thinking instead of looking. "Roberto is an FBI agent and private detective and is an expert at finding missing persons ..."

"Whoa, Chiche," I interrupted. "I'm an *ex*-FBI agent and an *ex*-private investigator. I'm now a writer, a writer of children's books. I wish I could convince you of that once and for all."

"Oh, I'm convinced, darling. It's just that I happen to know that you will sometimes use your expertise to help people in trouble — special people, I mean, like that poor woman whose retarded son was murdered, or when you found that horrible Nazi person."

By then it wasn't hard to deduce that Mireya was another "special person" who needed my help. I had sworn to myself that I would not get involved in any more criminal stuff, wouldn't even listen to potential clients. That's my weakness: once I agree to "just listen, please", I am often hooked. Mireya was now gazing at me through her emerald eyes with new interest.

"Now I really must get back to the meeting, but I want you to tell Roberto *every*thing, Mireya," Chiche said, "and I mean everything. And you, Roberto, just listen, please." She downed her *cafecito* in one gulp and started to put some money on the table, but I stopped her. It was only a gesture anyway.

Mireya and I were left looking at each other. "I don't want to inconvenience you, Roberto," Mireya said. "Chiche is trying to be helpful, but she has no right dragging other people into my problems."

I would do anything for you short of murder, my lovely child, I thought, but said, "It's all right. I'm listening."

Her husband, Pablo Calderón, had walked out of the house one Sunday morning a few months previously and never came back. I don't adhere to the let-it-all-out school of interrogation because it's a waste of time, so I ask questions.

"Did you go to the police?"

"Finally, yes, although I was hesitant to do so."

"Do you mean in case he'd been kidnapped?"

"No, if I thought that I'd have gone right to the police."

"Why then?"

"Because he might have been abducted by aliens and I didn't think it would be a good idea to tell the police that."

"You were right." I had been taking notes. Now I closed the notebook and put away my pen. I should have known she was too good to be true. Screwballs, beautiful or not, bore me. "Please explain," I said, resigned.

She smiled sadly, probably noticing my skepticism. "This wasn't the first time he'd disappeared. About a month before that he disappeared, but it was only for a week and I hadn't even noticed it." She had been looking down at her coffee cup and now looked up to see if I was still there. I was. "Why not?"

"He was supposed to be in Europe on business, but when he returned home he told me he had been abducted by aliens and they took him somewhere, another planet he supposed, and asked him a lot of questions and did some medical experiments, nothing invasive, blood and urine tests, things like that."

"So he never got to Europe?"

"No."

"And you bought that story?"

"Did you see the movie?"

"No, I read the book."

"So did I, the movie's better."

I had to smile. "I believe you." She smiled back, then laughed.

"Why are you laughing?" I asked.

"I don't know."

"Maybe because it sounds so ridiculous."

Her smile disappeared. "Yes, maybe that's why. But *is* it ridiculous? I mean, he's gone again."

"Yes, that part is true," I admitted. "Can you think of any reason why he'd *want* to be gone again?"

"Like another woman, for example?"

"For example."

"If so I don't know about it, and no one I know does either."

"How about work, money, mid-life crisis, anything like

that? Has he been acting strangely?"

"Actually yes, he's been quite nervous lately, but I attributed it to the ... er ... abduction."

"Sure. Anyone who's been abducted by aliens would feel nervous. There's one problem."

"Yes, Roberto?" she asked, leaning forward so her breasts were half exposed beneath a button that had come undone. I had been about to say that the alien abduction stories are pure bullshit and if she wanted my help she'd have to get that out of her system right now — as I would have said to any other client. But I melted before the flame of her beauty and couldn't do it. I said something about the abduction story being dubious, in my opinion, and that I preferred to concentrate on other aspects.

"Then you will help, Roberto? Oh, I'm so grateful."

"I feel privileged to be able to help, Mireya," I said, feeling like an idiot, but I was sincere, she had really gotten to me.

"How much do you charge, Roberto?" She blushed wonderfully. "Not that it matters, but I do want you to know that I'm able to pay whatever ..."

"Expenses, and they can add up," I said too quickly, and knew that I had it bad. I was sweating.

"I ... I don't know what to say." Her eyes were starting to be teary, so I decided to call it a day. "I'd like to come by your place tomorrow, if that's possible. I want to see where you live and ask a lot of questions; it's too late for that now." I wanted to examine my feelings as well.

I was at her house in San Isidro, an upper-class suburb of Buenos Aires, at nine the next morning, a Sunday. We sat on a veranda at the back looking onto an immense, tree and flower populated lawn. Mireya was dressed in shorts and a sleeveless t-shirt, no bra. Her indefinable hair, let out, sparkled in the sun, which was well over the trees in the east. Coffee, orange juice and croissants were laid out on a cloth-covered table. I had expected no less and so had not had breakfast at home.

"I'm fascinated by your history, Roberto," Mireya said. "FBI agent, private investigator, now author. Did you change because the FBI doesn't respect human rights?"

"Actually, the FBI does respect human rights, Mireya — too much so according to certain opinions. You're confusing them with the CIA, who are the bad guys in that respect."

"And you're the good guys?" she said in accent-free English, surprising me.

"Mostly, not always, but mostly," I answered in the same language.

"Are you Argentine or American?" she asked. "I can't tell by your speech?" I now noticed a slight accent in her speech though.

"Both. I was born in Buenos Aires, American father, Argentine mother. My father registered me at the U.S. consulate, so I became a citizen of both countries at birth. I went to college in the States, later I got into the FBI by accident because I needed a job after military service, spoke Spanish so they sent me here."

"I didn't know the FBI has people here."

"Then there's a lot you don't know." That sounds harsh, but I said it with a lopsided grin, so she just shrugged. "What about you?" I said, "I mean a short bio."

"Okay, but you forgot a detail in yours."

"An important one? I left out a lot of details."

"Are you married?"

"Oh that. Glad you're interested. But no, not at the moment."

"But you were," she insisted.

"Yes, but that was a long time ago. Can't we change the subject?"

She laughed. "Sure we can. I've found out all I wanted to know." I let that go, not wanting to rush things, but don't think it didn't excite me or that I didn't blush.

"How long have you been married, Mireya?" I asked, business-like.

"Five years." She needed no prompting. "I went to St. John's all the way through high school. Do you know what that is?"

"Very posh bilingual?"

"Exactly, explains my English, which you were probably wondering about."

"Yes, but your accent isn't really Anglo-Argentine."

"I went to college in England. My Dad wanted me to in order not to lose my Queen's English, Argentine version, of which he doesn't speak a word by the way. I met Pablo there, we got married and returned to Argentina when the dirty war ended. So I never got my degree."

"In what?"

"Theater."

"And now?"

"Housewife."

"Happily married housewife?"

She shrugged. "Pablo is very good to me, but San Isidro ain't Greenwich Village."

"Indeed it ain't. I'm originally from New York myself."

"She arched her eyebrows theatrically: Really? Anywhere near the Village?"

"Brooklyn."

Obviously disappointed, she could only say, "Oh, that's nice."

"Argentine men have a penchant for mistresses. Did Pablo ...?"

"Don't most men," she interrupted, "if they can afford it?"

"I guess so," I admitted, "but here it's pretty much an accepted way of life. What I'm getting at is whether your marriage was shaky for that reason or some other."

"Well," she said, "first of all I don't know if Pablo had a mistress." (She sounded offended, as most women will, whether they really care or not.) "And if our marriage was shaky (I noted the past tense), I'd say that it had cooled off considerably, but no more than that of most of my friends."

"Any children?"

"No."

"By choice?"

I could see I had hit a nerve. She looked at her fingernails, short ones attached to slender lightly freckled fingers, but wasn't seeing them. Finally she looked up and answered: "Not by my choice, but Pablo said he wasn't ready, he traveled a lot and so on. I asked when he'd be ready, I'm thirty-two for gods sake."

A frustrated suburban housewife, I thought. So what else is now? But she wasn't only that. I asked what she was doing now, she was working and acting in a Buenos Aires repertory theater. When I asked if it was the Suburban Players, an awful English-speaking amateur group, she glared and shot out, "God no! It's purely Argentine, in San Telmo."

"What's your attitude towards anthroposophy?" I asked, just from curiosity.

"It's marvelous!" she replied. "Although the people often give me a pain in the arse. Not Chiche of course, she's a darling. But you know … it … it gives life a meaning, and that's something lacking in a lot of people now, I know it was lacking in me. How about you?"

"I haven't really decided yet," I said, which was true enough. "And your husband, Pablo?"

"Oh, he thought it's all nonsense, for him if you can't see something through a telescope or a microscope or touch it, it's not there. You know what I mean."

"I do," I said, and decided she was warmed up enough to answer personal practical questions. "What are you doing for money now that your husband is no longer around? Or do you have your own?"

"No, I don't have any money of my own. You probably thought I did, having gone to St. John's and all, but my father went broke during one of Argentina's periodic economic crises, and they had to forgive the senior year's tuition. I went to college with an academic scholarship." She waited a moment for my next question, but I didn't ask it, knowing she'd go on. "After college I went to New York and waited tables, worked in hotels, sales clerk, that kind of thing. I love New York, I even became a Mets fan." (A girl after my heart.)

"You really were integrated then."

"Yes, I love baseball and hate soccer."

"And money now?" I asked, getting back on track.

"We have what I thought was a joint account, Pablo and I."

"What's not joint about it?" I asked, although I thought I already knew.

"I can draw money and write checks, but I can't get any information about the account."

"Is it called a special checking account?"

"Yes, that's it. I only found this out when I asked for the balance at the bank."

"And they told you that you aren't one of the account's title holders but have a special power to draw from it."

She nodded.

"How about credit cards?"

"I have Visa and American Express and I use them."

"Who pays the bills?"

"I don't know. They're in Pablo's name."

"Well, if there are computers on Mars, he could be paying them by internet."

She didn't smile.

"Sorry, I said, couldn't resist."

"So you definitely discard the abduction?"

"I never held it to discard. Your husband is either dead, kidnapped or running."

"Running?" She said, genuinely surprised. "From what?"

"You for instance. With all respect, Mireya, husbands have been known to run from their wives. Or something more serious like the police or the Mafia. What business is he in?"

"He's a trader."

"Of what?"

"Anything, commodities mostly, but also gold, silver, dollars, euros."

"How about drugs?"

"I don't think so. He never used drugs."

The doorbell — gate bell really — rang. The gate is a good football field away from the house. "Excuse me," Mireya said, and she walked into the living room where she pressed an intercom button. "Yes?"

"Está la Señora Calderón?" a tinny voice with a strange accent asked.

"Sí, soy yo."

I have a message from your man, Señora. (He said "hombre" instead of "marido" — husband.)

"He says he is fine and you should not worry." She turned and looked at me. I went quickly to her side,

"Where is he?" she asked

"He is very far away — with us."

She didn't need my prodding. "And who are *you*?" I opened the front door and ran down the entrance road toward the gate. There was no one there. I ran back. They were still talking.

"But when will he be back?"

"He does not know."

"Can you at least tell me if it will be soon?"

"No, he does not know yet. You are not to worry."

"*When* will he know?" she shouted.

"Good bye, sweetheart."

"What?"

"That's what he said." There was a click indicating the end of conversation.

"What did he say while I was out?" I asked Mireya.

She looked stunned. "When were you out?"

"You asked him who he is"

"Oh. He said he was a rep — rep, meaning representative I guess — of his galaxy. Did you see him?"

"At the gate? No, there was no one there. What galaxy?"

"He didn't say."

"Did you ask him?"

"No. Do you think you could find him if you knew the galaxy?"

I wasn't amused. "Is there another intercom, a box I mean, outside, at the back entrance?"

"The only entrance is at the front and there's no other intercom." She had reverted to Spanish.

I paced the living room and she sat, fell rather, into an armchair.

"Is it wireless?" I asked.

"What?"

"The intercom. Is it wireless?"

"Oh. Yes, it's wireless."

"It wouldn't be very difficult to hack it then."

"From another *galaxy*?"

I looked at her sharply to see if she was pulling my leg. I couldn't tell. "No — from a parked car around the corner, for example."

"Or another galaxy; they're very advanced, you know."

"Yes, I'm sure they are." I was getting exasperated, probably because the intercom bit shook me a little. "Look, Mireya, if Pablo was abducted and is being held on a small planet in a big galaxy, we won't find him. So I suggest we concentrate on the other alternatives."

"Okay," she smiled. She was a cool customer under the

circumstances. "Kidnapped?"

"Unlikely, they would have been after ransom long ago, unless they killed him by mistake."

"Oh, do you think so?"

"No, but it's happened. He could be dead, Mireya, you'll have to consider that. There are a lot of psychos in the world who kill for revenge or just for the hell of it. Did he have any enemies?"

"None that I know of," she said. "Actually he was very well liked."

"Do you have any pictures?"

She nodded and went into some other room. I went back to the veranda and finished my coffee, which was delicious be the way.

"Why, he looks like Cary Grant," I said when she showed me a photo of them both holding hands in front of what looked like a country hotel entrance.

"Yes, everyone says that, very handsome. He tried to get into the movies, but they said he looked too much like Cary Grant. Isn't that ironic? That's in La Cumbrecita, do you know it?"

"I've been there, yes, very faux-German."

"It is that, but beautiful, too. I love it there."

"One of my all-time favorite Cary Grant movies is *Gunga Din*," I said. Something was tickling my subconscious and I wanted to keep the conversation on Grant until it emerged, although *Gunga Din* really is one of my favorite movies.

"*Gunga Din*? I don't think I ever saw that one. I liked *An*

Affair to Remember best."

"How about Pablo, was he a Cary Grant fan?"

She thought a moment, then said, "Pablo liked to joke that he was just as handsome and would have been a better actor if he didn't look so much like him. He said he liked *Houseboat* best, but I think that was more because of Sophia Loren than Grant."

That was the moment of my inspiration, helped along by Mireya's comment and my having seen a documentary about Cary Grant on TV the night before.

"What was the date your husband disappeared, Mireya?" She told me. "May I use your phone?" I called Detective Comisario Alberto Contreras of the Argentine Federal Police. When he heard my voice he didn't exactly jump for joy: "*Puta*! Zorro, I hope you're calling to invite me for a game of chess and nothing to do with work. It's Sunday for the love of God." It was all a show we put on. Alberto helps me with information and sometimes strong-arm stuff, and I insure that he gets the police-side credit when investigations are successful. We are friends.

"No Sundays for a dedicated public asshole like you," I rejoined. "So please take a dozen aspirins to think straight for a change. I need information."

"Let me think, "he said, "Urgent? Yesterday?"

"Naturally. I need to find out if a Pablo Calderón left Argentina on September 30th or 31st ... no, or August 1st."

"By foot or balloon?"

"*Basta*, Alberto, by airplane. Try Rome first."

"What's in it for me?"

"Maybe nothing this time."

"Oh, a favor, eh?"

"Right. How many do you owe me?"

"Well, there was last September 31st..." I snorted into the phone.

"Okay, Roberto, I'll have to wake up that stupid Chief of the airport police and get him on it, then someone'll have to go through all the departures cards. Might take a while."

"Ten minutes will be fine." I hung up.

"Why Rome?" Mireya said.

"Just a hunch. How about taking a walk?"

Alberto knows a lot of people in police work, and most of them owe him; if he could get the information I suspected existed at the airport, I'd be owing him as well — but I'm used to that. My cell phone rang three hours later while Mireya and I were eating dessert at "La Tienda", a very good San Isidro restaurant. We'd downed a bottle of excellent Argentine wine and I felt like having a long siesta, preferably with Mireya by my side — but it was not to be.

"You're in luck, Zorro," Alberto growled. "The card was in the first pile they checked. Your boy left for Rome on Aerolíneas Argentinas flight 1344 on August 1st."

"I don't suppose they checked if he came back," I said. "I forgot to mention that."

"Please kiss my ass the first chance you get." And he hung up, smiling I was sure.

I looked at my watch, then at Mireya. "Came back ...?" She said.

"What are you doing tonight, Mireya?"

"Tonight? Why I ..."

"How'd you like to accompany me to Rome?"

"He went to Rome?"

"That's right, unless there's another Pablo Calderón who departed by Aerolíneas Argentinas flight 1344 to Rome the day after your husband, Pablo Calderón, disappeared."

"*Hijo de puta!*"

"Indeed."

"You knew he went to Rome, Roberto. How?"

"Just a guess that turned out to be right."

"All right, how did you guess right then?"

"You're not going to like it, Mireya."

"Tell me."

"Okay." I reverted to English, which I often do, even thinking, when something gets delicate. "Pablo is the spitting image of Cary Grant, right?"

"Spitting image?"

"He looks just like him."

She nodded.

"Did anyone ever tell you that you look like Betsy Drake?"

"No, I never heard of her."

"She was before your time. Anyway, she was an actress

who didn't do many films and she was Cary Grant's third wife."

"Third? How many did he have?"

"Five. And you do look like her." I waited for it to sink in.

"Very well, so what?" She was staying in Spanish, so a bilingual conversation ensued.

"But you do know who Sofia Loren is."

"Of course — and I don't look like her."

"Betsy Drake was originally cast for the part in *Houseboat*," I explained, "but they changed to Sofia, who was a much bigger name. Personally I think she was miscast. Anyway, Cary fell in love with Sofia and they had an affair. Betsy had accompanied him to Italy and when she noticed something going on, and still smarting from having been rejected for the role, she was furious and took the next boat home."

Mireya frowned: "How do you know all this, Roberto?"

"I saw a biography of Cary Grant on Film & Arts last night after leaving you."

"On *tele*vision?"

"Well, I wasn't there." Silence. "Look, you asked me how I got the idea of Rome ..."

"Yes, sorry. Go on."

"So I figured that if the new Cary Grant, now Pablo Calderón, is now married to someone who reminds him of Betsy Drake — are you sure he never mentioned that?"

She downed the remains of her wine. "Now that you

mention it, maybe he did. I don't remember the name, just Cary Grant's wife."

"You see, Cary stayed in Italy after the filming, trying to keep the affair with Sofia going, but she tried to break it off. He kept after her though, until she finally married Carlo Ponti, about the most un-Cary Grant like guy you can imagine."

"Roberto!" Her eyes gleamed with what looked like amusement.

"Yes?"

"Are you suggesting that Pablo — my Pablo — went to Rome after Sofia Loren. My god, she must be ancient!"

"Not necessarily, but maybe someone like her." That wasn't true. I had been thinking of Sofia Loren. In that same Cary Grant bio, they interviewed Sofia Loren about him *now*. She's seventy-one and doesn't look a day over forty and is still as beautiful as ever.

"Look, Mireya, that just gave me the hunch, which might be all wet ..."

"All wet?"

"Wrong. All we really know is that a guy with Pablo's name left for Rome on a particular day, and it looks like it was your husband. Hunches are funny things, they're like intuition. If they're wrong, you can spend a hell of a lot of time on wild goose chases. If they're right though — and my hunches are usually more right than wrong — you're in business a lot sooner than you normally would be. So, what are you doing tonight?"

"Tonight? Why I'm going to Rome with you to look for that *hijo de puta*. Sofia Loren indeed. What time does the flight leave?"

We went back to her house to order electronic tickets via internet with her credit card. She didn't know how so I worked the computer. "I usually travel business class on business," I told her. She was standing next to me with her hip touching my shoulder. "Oh, let's go first class," she said and yawned. I then phoned the Plaza Hotel on the Via del Corso and reserved two single rooms for the next day. The Plaza is an insider's hotel, old fashioned, elegant, a few blocks from the Spanish Stairs. I always stayed there when I was working the FBI international beat.

"By the way," I asked the voice at the other end of the phone, "Is Signor Pablo Calderón still there?" I had no clue to indicate that he might have gone to that hotel, but if not, it would be one less place to look.

Silence as the voice worked its computer, then, "No, he must have checked out."

"Oh, do you remember him then?"

"No, but if he was here and isn't now he must have checked out, *ne's pas*?"

Wise guy. "Si, grazie."

Then I called a contact in the anti-terrorism police in Rome and asked him to check arrivals from Buenos Aires on Aerolíneas Argentinas flight 1344 on September 1 and tell me the local address he gave. The Italians have all that stuff computerized, so it shouldn't take them long. I don't know if he knew that I was no longer FBI and I didn't tell him. I think he'd have done me the favor anyway. He owed me one. He called me on my cellphone when we were in the airport. "Hotel Plaza, Via del Curso, Roberto," he said.

During the flight to Rome I lifted the armrest between us out of the way and Mireya slept with her head on my shoulder. Like a baby. I sleep badly on airplanes, so I consciously enjoyed that. Her hair changed from chocolate to strawberry when the first rays of the morning sun crept through the plastic shutters on the windows and tousled it.

Old time European hotel concierges have a well-trained gift for remembering names and faces. I'm also good at faces, but a failure at names. When we walked into the Plaza Hotel on Monday morning the concierge looked at me and said, "Signor Fox, so nice to see you again. It's been years." He must have checked the reservation list and recognized my name; it's unlikely that even Pietro — according to his name plate — would have immediately been able to remember both my face and name if he hadn't been expecting me.

"It's good to see you, too, Pietro. And yes it's been years, many years. I congratulate you on your memory."

"Where distinguished guests are concerned, my memory is also distinguished," he said with a huge smile which revealed his gold tooth. That I remembered. He looked at Mireya appreciatively. "You reserved two single rooms, Signor Fox. Am I correct?" — as though there must have been some mistake. I acknowledged that strange truth and turned to Mireya. "You can go right up if you wish, dear, I'll take care of the formalities." Pietro, not missing a beat, took two adjoining keys (not electronic cards) from the key-box and rang the bell for a boy, who appeared like a genii at our side. Pietro gave him one of the keys and Mireya followed him to the elevator. "I'll be right up." I told her.

I filled out the registration card as man and wife quickly and handed it to the concierge along with a hundred euro bill. He didn't blink, waiting to hear what I wanted. "Can we talk somewhere privately, Pietro?" I asked him. Several people were behind me waiting to register.

"But of course." He snapped his fingers at a young assistant doing paper work at a desk behind him. "Take over, Giuseppe." He came from behind the counter and led me to a small alcove near the elevators and out a door into a side street, where he took a foul Italian black cigarette and lit up. "What can I do for you, Signor Roberto?" Corruption breeds familiarity.

"I'm looking for someone you may know or remember, Pietro. As you know, I have great respect for your memory."

He smiled. "It is magnificent, I admit, but not infallible like the Pope's. Who is it?"

"Cary Grant."

He coughed on the smoke he had just inhaled and looked at me as one who has heard everything might. "But of course I remember him. He always stayed here when he was in Rome, in the Presidential suite. A great gentleman and a wonderful tipper. But alas, Signor Roberto, you must know that he is dead."

"Yes, I know that, but actually I'm looking someone who looks very much like him, an Argentine named Calderón."

"Calderone? Yes, you are right, he is a dead ringer."

"Then you do know him. But it's Calderón."

"No, Calderone — Conde Paolo Calderone. I am sure. And if he is Argentine, I never heard one speak such perfect

Italian."

Now I looked at him as one who thought he had heard everything. "Count?"

Pietro laughed. "That's what he says, and we never question titles here; we welcome them."

"Is he still here?"

"In the hotel? No, he stayed for a few days a month or two ago, then left for his castle, or manor, wherever counts live."

"I see. And do you know how I can find him?"

He scratched his head and looked at the sky. "It's possible."

I handed him another hundred euros. "Probable?"

He looked at his watch. "Definitely. Tonight in our private dining room at ten o'clock, where he will likely be accompanied by Sofia Loren."

I assumed he was using the name ironically, as I had used Cary Grant's. "Ah," I said, "a Sofia Loren look-alike."

"Look-alike? No, Signor Roberto, la Loren herself, in the flesh."

I couldn't believe my luck. "Pietro, you are a genius."

"Perhaps, but there is a complication. You see, there will be ten people, important men with their wives or paramours, including our Prime Minister. They come in and leave through a side door and there is obviously a lot of security. Berlusconi is not very popular, you know ... and you and Signora Fox are not invited."

I thought about this a moment, then said, "Complications can be simplified with planning and good will." [and money] "Could I get a message to ... er ... the count at an appropriate moment?"

I wanted Mireya to identify our Count Calderone before confronting him. I told her what the concierge had revealed and outlined my plan. I wrote a note in Spanish:

Sr. Pablo Calderón: My name is Roberto Fox and I am a friend of your wife's. I would like to invite you for a drink. I am in hotel's Garibaldi Bar wearing a New York Mets cap ... to be given to the count at dessert.

Mireya would be in the bar at a table in the rear with a wide-brimmed hat covering most of her face and stuffing in her clothing to make her look fat. When Pablo walked in and approached me, she would stand up and leave if she was sure it was him and remain seated if it wasn't him or if she wasn't sure. I would watch her in the mirror. It would also cost. She gave me five hundred euros, two hundred to cover what I had already paid Pietro and another three for the head waiter to pass the note.

It worked perfectly. At midnight Count Calderone walked into the bar and spotted me immediately wearing the ridiculous cap I had bought in a kiosk across from the hotel, looking like a typical American tourist. I watched fat Mireya put down her third martini, stand and stagger dumpishly out.

"Signor Fox?" he asked.

"Señor Calderón," I replied in Spanish. "What are you drinking?" The bartender had come over.

"Brandy, you interrupted mine at dinner, he said in the same language." He waited until the bartender poured his

Napoleon then said, "Who are you?"

"My name is really Roberto Fox and I'm a private investigator."

"Ah, for Calderón's wife."

I almost smiled at the impertinence. "For *your* wife, Calderón." The resemblance to Cary Grant was uncanny, but his voice was different, high-pitched, and he didn't walk jauntily bow-legged like Grant.

"You are mistaken, Fox ..."

"She just identified you positively."

"She's here?"

"She just walked out, disguised so you wouldn't recognize her."

"You needn't have gone to the trouble; I wouldn't have recognized her anyway."

"Come on, Calderón," I said. "What's the game?"

"No game, it's very serious. Pablo Calderón is very far away, farther than you can imagine ..."

"I already saw that movie ..."

"Just be quiet a moment and I'll explain," he said angrily. "If you don't want to hear me out I'll leave and you won't live to see another Roman morning."

I didn't ask if that was a threat, there was no mistaking it, and I must admit to having a sense of fear. After all, this guy was hobnobbing with some of the biggest crooks in Italy, where they know how to breed them. I was quiet.

"As I said, Calderón is far away, safe and content on a

planet, *my* planet."

"In another galaxy?" I was about to wisecrack about him cavorting with virgins up there but kept it to myself.

"Well, just between you and me it's the same galaxy in another universe. Meanwhile I inhabit his body in order to carry out intensive research here on your earth." He paused, to let it sink in I suppose, which it didn't, quite.

"What kind of research? Did you ask, 'Take me to your leader' and they showed you Berlusconi, for god's sake?"

He smiled. "For starters, yes. There are many others, of course."

"George W., for example?"

"I do expect to be introduced to him shortly, yes."

"After the Italian movie stars."

"They can open many doors."

"But what's the point, Pablo?"

"You may call me Paolo, Roberto." He was warming up. How people like to talk about themselves! "If you mean what is the objective of my research, please believe that we have no intention of invading your planet ..."

"Well, *that's* a relief."

"You see, I'm writing a novel."

For the first time I began to take him seriously. "About the earth?"

"Yes, a historical novel."

"Uh huh, and how long will it take, I mean how long will

Calderón be away?"

"My sabbatical is for seven years."

"I see. And then you'll be Calderón again?"

"Señor Calderón has signed a contract which stipulates that he will stay on our planet for seven years. After the expiration date of the contract he may return or stay where he is, as he wishes."

"What do you think he'll do?"

"That's hard to say. If I were him though, considering what I've seen here so far, I'd stay there."

"What's your planet's name?" I asked stalling for time in the hope of thinking of something more intelligent.

"You couldn't pronounce it. Look, Mrs. Calderón has nothing to worry about. Her husband's fortune is at her disposal and she can do anything she likes. Why don't you tell her that, Roberto?" He smiled a Cary Grant smile.

"What if she wants to expose you? No one will believe the abduction story. And your DNA is still Calderón's."

The smile disappeared. "You still don't understand, do you? Let me make the situation as clear as possible. One: the first time was indeed what you call an abduction. The second time, however, Pablo went willingly with us. In fact, he wanted to come. Two: This body's DNA no longer matches Calderón's; we think of everything and changing DNA — temporarily — is child's play for us. Three: You'd be surprised at how many people would believe the abduction story. In fact, most of Pablo's friends and relatives already do. Four: I much prefer that Mrs. Calderón not denounce anything because it would result in publicity which I want to avoid.

Five: Since you — and I assume soon Mrs. Calderón — are the only ones on earth who know the facts, I hold you personally responsible for not revealing them to anyone else. Is that a threat? you are thinking. The answer is yes. Have I made myself clear or must I put it even more simply?"

I ignored the sarcasm. "Just one question. How can Calderón be on your unpronounceable planet if his body is here?"

He smiled again, possibly because he recognized that the question was serious. "Good question, Roberto. You may know that human beings (and we are also human beings) are composed of body, soul and spirit ..."

"I've heard that, yes."

"Good. Pablo's soul and spirit are on planet xxxxx." He was right, I couldn't pronounce or understand it.

"In your body?"

"Of course."

"Does he look like Cary Grant there, too?"

He laughed out loud. "Good heavens no. I've been told I resemble Brad Pitt." He looked at his watch, a Rolex I noticed. "Now I must really go back to my party. They'll have already handed out the Havana *puros* and I've developed a taste for them." He held out his hand, which I took. "*Arrivederchi*, Roberto Fox. It's been a pleasure meeting you — *for the first and last time.*"

I knocked on Mireya's door. She had unstuffed herself and looked lovely in a knee-length, low-cut blue dress that still had the label attached; she must have bought it this afternoon. "Open the minibar, Mireya," I said. "We need a drink." While we sipped our Dewar's scotch, I told her the whole conversation I'd just had with ... whoever.

She sat still for a while, then crossed and re-crossed her legs twice, then asked, "Do you think he was telling the truth?"

"No ... but, oh hell, I don't know. What do you think?"

"What do I think?" She uncrossed her legs, stood up and smiled deliciously as her hair slowly turned dark red. "I think we should move to a double room."

"We are the lucky ones ..."

by Z

Translated by Frank Thomas Smith

When I moved *with my family to the country from Buenos Aires 14 years ago, we lived in an old house, once the core building of an estancia. There were ten acres of what was once farmland, but had turned into what my son, ten years old at the time, rather romantically and with his flair for exaggeration called a jungle. After a few days of snooping around in the "jungle" with his dog, he found a rusty old lunch pail. It had no lock on it, but it was rusted tightly shut, so he brought it to me to open, which I did with the help of a chisel and hammer. Instead of a rotted chicken leg, we found a ... what should I call it? An essay, or simply an unfinished manuscript. Translated into English, it reads as follows.*

We were four or five men, all about the same age, in our early forties, except for Dr. Bernard Lievegoed, who was in his mid-sixties then, and Lex Bos, seven years older than I. We were of different nationalities — I remember a Swiss who lived in Sao Paulo, Brazil, a German who lived in Johannesburg, South Africa. The others were Europeans, if I remember correctly. And I, an Argentine who was about to escape from my own country to Spain. Lievegoed and Bos were Dutch, and we were in the Dutch city of Zeist, at the headquarters of NPI — the Netherlands Pedagogic Institute.

In spite of its name, NPI was — and still is — a consulting firm. Bernard Lievegoed, a physician and psychiatrist, was its founder. At that time, 1974, it was called NPI International, because of its intention to expand its network around the world. In fact, that's what we were doing there. Lievegoed gave a kind of introductory talk. He started off by saying: "We are the lucky ones ..."

I can't say that I had been "recruited" by Lex Bos, because keeping one's eye out for potential co-workers isn't the same thing. Furthermore, I probably asked him about joining NPI rather then his asking me if I wanted to. At the time I had what many considered a good job — as an investigator for IATA, the International Air Transport Association — and senior man in Argentina. But I was just at that age when grown men buy their first motorcycles and change wives. Furthermore, Argentina was being terrorized by leftist revolutionaries, specifically the *Ejército Revolucionario del Pueblo,* which specialized in kidnapping business executives. My colleagues, the airline managers, had moved their offices across the Rio de la Plata to Montevideo, in Uruguay. You see, the possibility of being kidnapped for ransom and political statement was quite real. I felt that the work I was doing was not worth it. Something else influenced my decision; in fact, it was the main reason: anthroposophy.

The first time I'd heard of it was when I was a student in Germany. My future wife's aunt and uncle were anthroposophists and they told me about it during several conversations about things existential. What interested me about it was that it included the idea of reincarnation, yet was philosophically western; that is, it's founder and principal protagonist was Rudolf Steiner, an Austrian philosopher and esotericist.

I found work with Argentine Airlines in Germany without having finished my studies in business administration. After a few years, I was included in the airline's management training program and transferred to head office in Buenos Aires. By that time, I was married and had a three-year-old daughter. We found a small house in a Buenos Aires suburb called Florida, at that time still heavily populated by German immigrants — including Jews and Nazis, who seemed to get along rather well there. The Nazis never admitted to having been of that persuasion of course. Three blocks from our home was the "Rudolf Steiner Schule". My wife was German, so that was our daughter's mother tongue, and I of course spoke German from my time in Germany, so it seemed practical to send the child to that school ... just to the kindergarten, I thought, because I intended to send her to an American or English primary school, English being, I felt, much more important for her future.

As it turned out though, my daughter loved the kindergarten and the whole school atmosphere impressed my wife and me so much, that we decided to let her continue in the primary school.

Steiner or Waldorf schools are based on anthroposophy, which reminded me of Aunt Trude and uncle Karl back in Frankfurt. But when I asked questions about anthroposophy in the Steiner Schule in Florida, I was referred to a priest in the Christian community — a church whose theology is based on Rudolf Steiner's teachings about Christianity. I soon found myself in a study group reading a series of Steiner lectures about "The Gospel of St. Luke" — in German of course. It floored me. I was born and raised Roman Catholic, but had moved away from the Church, mostly because of all the unanswered questions — the ones they answer by saying "it's a mystery" — which is, of course, no answer. Well, Steiner answered them all, or most all. Not only religious questions though.

Due to a crisis in the Rudolf Steiner School when my daughter was in the second grade, a group of parents took our kids out and started a new school, a new Waldorf school, as best we could. So I got more and more deeply involved — as president of the Board and teacher of English — one hour a day, so I kept my day job. I realized that the Waldorf educational system, based on anthroposophy, provides the spiritual and artistic warmth children need, something different than what the mainstream schools practice. And it works, the children are happy, and they thrive.

Steiner also wrote a book about "the social question". He was talking about his time of course, but there is much in it that is applicable today: "Basic Issues of the Social Question." I read it during the Cold War, when the duality of capitalism-communism dominated the political-social scene. Here, I thought, was a "third way". What also impressed me was that the same guy who went on and on about the spiritual world, initiation, science and religion, was also into politics and economics.

So when Bernard Lievegoed in Holland said: "We are the lucky ones ..." and ended the sentence with, "... for we have anthroposophy, and are therefore morally obliged to help the others, who do not have it," I was somewhat surprised that he included me in those who "had" anthroposophy, and it started me thinking about what that means. I'm still thinking about it and can at least say what he did *not* mean:

proselytizing. Lievegoed knew that anthroposophy is not for everyone. After all, according to Steiner, "Anthroposophy is a path of knowledge which would guide the spiritual in the human being to the spiritual in the cosmos. It manifests as a necessity of the heart and feeling. It must find its justification in being able to satisfy this need ..."

For me this meant answering certain existential questions, such as, *Does life have meaning?* (If not, what's the point? If so, what *is* that meaning?) I think that Rudolf Steiner answered these questions. The answer to the first question is: Yes! If proof is needed, well, just look around — at nature, where we see evidence of intelligence. Nature is intelligence, and very beautiful, and efficient, even when "red in tooth and claw". So if intelligence exists in nature, some intelligent being or beings must have put it there. Nothing could be more logical. Spontaneous intelligence is no more possible than spontaneous life is. The only intelligent beings, and by that I mean *thinking* beings, are humans. Yet human beings do not create nature, they are born into it. Steiner maintained that nature is a solidified spiritual substance, that everything which exists in the physical world also exists (or pre-exists) in the spiritual world in spiritual form and spiritual beings are the artistic creators of the Earth and nature.

The main question, then, is whether a spiritual world that cares about human beings really exists. Can we assume that man, a thinking being — when thinking is a spiritual activity and therefore intimately related to the spiritual world — was created in order to live a life without meaning? Well yes, we can assume that. I, however, prefer to side with Kierkegaard and insist — if only to myself — on the absurdity of meaningless human life.

The next question we face is: What *is* that meaning?

We know that life is often — or mostly — cruel and unjust. But not always! It can also be gentle and beautiful, with traces of love. Steiner maintained that we are living on a planet, Earth, of love. That is , the mission of the earth is to *become* a planet of love. Obviously, that will take a long time, and it's not a guaranteed outcome. It requires development — or evolution if you prefer — of consciousness and knowledge. And, most of all, *freedom*. Love is not possible without freedom. So, the reason, the meaning of life, is to develop love and freedom despite all the material and spiritual obstacles.

If we have convinced ourselves that life is meaningful and there is a spiritual intelligence behind it, then how do we explain the often horrible injustices occurring daily in the world, sometimes due to natural causes, but more often to human depravity? The only explanation is reincarnation. A dead and/or tortured child can hardly be the end-product of spiritual intelligence and justice. No, the child must have an ongoing opportunity to live and evolve — despite death! That can often only happen in a future incarnation on earth. Dostoyevsky's Ivan in *The Brothers Karamazov* famously does not kill God, like Nietzsche, that is, consider Him dead or non-existent, but rejects Him because he allows the suffering of children. Ivan did not consider reincarnation when condemning God and his holy Russian monk.

If there is reincarnation, there must also be karma — the retribution for the suffering you've caused — and compensation for the suffering you have undergone, but not necessarily during the same lifetime.

Then there is also "egotistical karma" — which provides

practical reasons for helping the poor and for saving the planet. India, (for example) presently has 1.2 billion people, most of them poor. And other parts of the world, including Latin America, are also mostly poor. As long as such large majorities remain poor, there is much more chance of us being poor in future incarnations. Or having to live on a polluted planet. The possibility even exists of there not being a planet to incarnate onto. Endgame ...?

The manuscript ends there. I do not know why it was hidden in a lunchpail and left in the valley of Traslasierra, so far from Buenos Aires. It is unsigned, so I don't even know who wrote it — in longhand, by the way. So I just call him "Z". After translating it, I looked into anthroposophy myself, if only because Z was so enthusiastic about it. I found it quite interesting and have even devoted a section of Southern Cross Review to it. Z would be happy about that, I feel sure.

FTS

by Roberto Fox

Evermore

And the Raven, never flitting, still is sitting, still is sitting,
And his eyes have all the seeming of a demon's that is dreaming,
And the lamp-light o'er him streaming throws his shadow on the floor;
And my soul from out that shadow that lies floating on the floor
Shall be lifted — nevermore!

From "The Raven" by Edgar Allen Poe

I went to the school that Sunday afternoon because there was a Board meeting that evening and we'd need some papers from the office. The secretary was ill though; nothing serious, but she wouldn't be able to attend the meeting, so I, living close, went to the school to get the necessary papers. There were no classes on Sunday, no children running about and calling out, so everything was unnaturally still. But I better start at the beginning to show you why I am in this remote place and what I have to do with the school.

*

I'm a journalist, which usually means frustrated writer, and certainly does in my case. I was born and raised in Buenos Aires, Argentina by my Anglo-Argentine parents. My great-grandparents were Anglos — great-grandfather British, great-grandmother American — and their descendants intermarried within the Anglo community, sent their kids to bilingual schools and spoke English at home. In a country like Argentina knowing English fluently Is a great advantage because foreign companies, be they American, British or

Japanese, need bilingual people. So when I finished university, I got a job right off with PanAm (since defunct) as a ticket agent at the airport, despite having studied literature and philosophy. Actually, it was fun and was a great opportunity to meet lovely, "free-thinking" girls — at that time still a rarity in Argentina — especially flight attendants.

But I got bored after a while and went to work for the *Buenos Aires Herald*, a pretty good English language daily which won fame as the only Argentine newspaper that wrote the truth during the military dictatorship — in power when Argentina won the soccer World Cup. There was no overt censorship, I mean you didn't have to submit your editions to the government before printing. No, their method was fear. Every owner, editor and reporter of the Spanish language publications knew that if they printed something the junta didn't like their life would be in serious danger. There had been one courageous magazine that tried to tell it like it was and the owner-editor was tortured before his planned assassination, but pressure from abroad, mostly from the Carter administration, saved his life and they gave him a one-way ticket to the States and a warning never to come back. The Herald paid less than PanAm, but I didn't need much, and it was what I wanted to do.

The junta figured that they should leave the *Buenos Aires Herald* alone because of its contacts with the U.S. and British embassies, as well as the fact that only foreigners and Anglo-Argentines read it. But it finally became too influential abroad, with stories being reprinted in the New York Times and the Washington Post, among others, so our masters decided that enough was enough. A few anonymous phonecalls to the editor and his wife did the trick. Not that he was a coward, quite the contrary, he had printed really inflammatory stuff as far as the junta was concerned. But a threatening phone call from someone you know is serious and quite capable of eliminating your family one by one by "disappearing" them is different from a bluff. So, the editor, an American (anyone interested can find out his name easily), finally decided it wasn't worth it, and accepted a job as editor of a newspaper in North Carolina. He asked me to come along. I hadn't been threatened directly, but some of my articles were the most damning — along with his editorials of course. He assured me I'd be next and recommended that I get out while I was still alive because as an unknown outside Argentina, they might not even bother to warn me first.

So, I wound up in North Carolina, but didn't stay there long. New York City beckoned. I got a job as a reporter for Newsday, the Long Island daily, which had won a couple of Pulitzer Prizes. It was considered a steppingstone to the Times. I fell in love and married the assistant editor, which was a mistake, probably because an Argentine macho simply can never get used to living with his female boss. There were other reasons of course, but I'll leave it at that. As correspondent for the paper, I was able to travel to various continents and countries, which I wrote about authoritatively, but learned that you can never really know anything about what's going on without having lived in the place for at least a couple of years and speak the language. But I'm digressing.

Finally, I wrote a book, a novel with Argentina and Chile as background. I can give aspiring writers some advice based on that experience. Getting a book published is harder than writing it. So, the best opening is to know someone in publishing — or know someone who knows someone. My wife — ex-wife, that is — knew someone and the book got published. It didn't sell very many copies, the fate of most books, but it at least gave me a literary biography. Also, if you are from a third-world country, or can pretend to be, it's a big help. And the more miserable the country the better. You can get speaking engagements at universities, some of which pay very well. An accent helps, something I don't have naturally, but it's easy to put one on, however slight. I was invariably asked when my second book would appear. My answer was that I didn't have time to write it. This is a great opening for a grant, which I received from a do-gooder foundation. (I'm getting to the point, don't worry.)

The grant would enable me to take a year off work to write my novel. In New York, though, I'd have to write it living in a one-room hovel a la Raskolnikov. In Argentina, because of the favorable exchange rate, I'd be comfortably ensconced in a three-room Buenos Aires apartment or a house in the hinterland. I decided on the latter. I should mention that during my absence the Falkland Islands war had taken place, the military junta deposed, and a semblance of democracy had returned.

An Argentine writer friend — a middle-aged lady who was an expert at milking the third-world angle, in fact I met her at a writers' colony in Iowa — suggested the Traslasierra Valley, a picturesque area five hundred miles west of Buenos Aires in the province of Córdoba. I remembered the name; I had gone there once as a child with my parents before they broke up. It seemed like fate, so that's where I went. I was able to rent a beautiful house with a hectare of garden and a swimming pool for three hundred bucks a month, which wouldn't have paid for a closet in Manhattan. I spent a week in Buenos Aires, my hometown, before going there, looked up old friends, especially girlfriends, but they were all married, marriage still being a big deal in Argentina, avoided relatives and finally boarded an Aerolíneas Argentinas plane for the one-hour flight to the city of Córdoba.

It was a workhorse Boeing 737 with six-seat-across rows. I chose a window seat near the front, because those are the best seats for short flights when the weather is good and there's something to see outside; they're the worst seats at night during long flights because you have to step over four legs to go to the toilette or stretch, so an aisle seat is preferable then. The worst is the middle seat, a.k.a. the squeeze-seat. I approached my window seat and wasn't too surprised, because it happens all the time, to see someone sitting in it. When you point out that they're in your seat, they feign surprise, look at their boarding pass, say "Oh!" or "Ah!" and wait for you to insist. They will have to squeeze out to the aisle, let you in, then go on back, usually to the squeeze-seat where they belong. A black man, Brazilian I assumed, with long legs was already seated in the aisle seat, which is where long legs belong, for they can stretch at least one out into the aisle once everyone is seated.

"This is your seat?" the young woman in the window-seat said, looking up at me with large, almond-shaped Audrey Hepburn eyes. She was more rounded than Hepburn, but almost as beautiful in a different way, with long black hair tied back with what I later saw to be a piece of red string. Her skin was dark, olive really, and she had high cheekbones and a delicate nose and a slightly jutting chin. "How do you know?"

she said with a smile revealing large white teeth, made whiter by her dark complexion.

"My boarding pass says so." I also smiled, already recognizing that this was someone I should get to know. I held out the pass with the window seat, 4F, plainly visible. She squinted at it and said, "Oh, I have one of those too." She started to rummage in her knapsack, which she'd hauled from under her seat. Meanwhile a line of passengers had backed up behind me waiting to pass. "Do you mind?" a sweating woman behind me asked. She was too fat to squeeze around me.

The black man, who turned out to be American, said, in English, "It's only an hour flight; cool it, man," assuming that I'd understand him. He hadn't understood a word of our short dialogue, but the situation was obvious.

"It's all right," I said to the young woman, "stay where you are." Then, to the American, in English, "Do you mind?" He stood up as far as he could, hunched over, and let me pass into the squeeze seat.

"I'm terribly sorry," the young woman said to me while I was buckling my seat belt, "the flight attendant showed me to this row, and I didn't realize the seats were numbered." She looked sincerely worried, and I believed her.

"Don't worry," I told her, "it's only an hour's flight."

"Are you sure you don't mind?"

"Absolutely sure."

"It's only and hour's flight, man," the black guy said, "you done the right thing. They couldna made these seats any smaller, could they?"

"You a basketball player?" I asked him.

"You got it — and I shoulda bought two seats. You ever hear of a team called 'Atenas'?"

"Yes, one of the best Argentine teams, from Córdoba. Is that who you're playing for?"

"Right, maybe Ginobili played for them?"

"I don't know, the last years before the NBA he was in Europe."

"Don't blame him. Europe pays better than here."

"But living costs are much higher there, so it probably works out the same," I consoled him. I like professional basketball, so the conversation wasn't uninteresting, but I wanted to turn my attention to the girl. "Well, good luck," I told him as we were taking off. I leaned toward her with the pretense of looking out the window. "Buenos Aires is a beautiful sight from the air," I said.

"Oh yes," she replied. "I never saw it before." She was clutching the arms of her seat, one of which we shared.

"Look," I said, extending my left arm in front of her, " there's the *obelisco*."

She laughed. "Small, isn't it?" We hit an air pocket and the plane jumped. I had slyly rested my arm on our shared armrest, so when her body stiffened, she grasped my wrist. I gently placed my hand over hers. She was so nervous she probably didn't even notice it. When the plane had passed through some bumpy clouds and reached cruising altitude and the sunlight, she let her breath out and withdrew her hand.

"I'm sorry," she said, smiling at me. "I've never flown before."

"I guessed that."

"Because I'm so nervous?"

"No, because you didn't know about the seat numbers. Do you live in Córdoba?"

"Not yet, and not in the city. But I will be living in the Province as soon as I get there." I had to think a moment to decipher that and when I did, I asked, "Really, where in the Province?" I was prepared to change my plans about going to live in Villa de las Rosas, despite having already paid a deposit on a house, and say that I was on my way to wherever she was going ... but I didn't have to. "Villa de las Rosas," she said. "It's a small town on the other side of the *Altas Cumbres*, I'm going to teach in a school there."

Some people say they don't believe in coincidences. I counted myself among those who do and persisted in that opinion even after this remarkable event. "What a coincidence!" I exclaimed.

"Not a coincidence really," she said. "I've been studying and preparing myself to teach in a school like that one for some time now. It's a wonderful opportunity."

"I'm sure it is, but I didn't mean that. You see, I'm also going to Villa de las Rosas where I don't live yet but will, once I get there."

"*Cielos*! If I believed in coincidences, I'd certainly agree that this is one," she said, smiling at me with those huge black eyes.

"But if you don't believe in coincidences, what is it?"

"Karma, or maybe just synchronicity."

That didn't surprise me at all; she had the slightly kooky look of a new Jungian innocence. "Ah yes," I said wisely, "karma."

After the flight we took a taxi to the bus terminal in Córdoba and from there a three-hour bus trip over the Sierra Grande to the Traslasierra Valley and the village of Villa de las Rosas. I paid for the taxi, but Mireya insisted on paying her own bus fare. We had a lot of time to talk and get to know each other.

"Do you think our meeting was karma?" I asked her as *El Petizo* — The Runt — our aptly named bus, groaned its way over the Sierra. A loaded question: women like to believe their love affairs are made by the stars, and I was already determined to turn our meeting into just that. Cynical I admit, and yet, well, you've heard of love at first sight and, corny as it sounds ... this was it.

Following script, she should now blush, look at me sideways, raise her eyebrows and shrug her shoulders coquettishly.

But she didn't do that. Instead, she looked me straight in the eye and said, "*Sí.*"

We arrived finally in Villa de las Rosas as the sun was setting, painting the Sierra behind us a rose color and I wondered if the town was named after the flower or the sunset. By then we had agreed that she would stay at my place (plenty of room, I'd insisted, which was true) until she found someplace to live. Her salary at the school was meager because she taught only two classes of painting a day because, she eventually admitted, she was still weak from a bout with cancer, now in remission. She did look for a place to rent but found nothing satisfactory within her means. I hoped she wasn't looking very hard, for I offered to let her stay with me; I wanted, in fact, very much for her to stay, and she knew it. Finally, she agreed to stay if she could pay rent. We both knew this was for appearance's sake.

She talked a lot about the school and the Weltanschauung behind it, which was something called anthroposophy or spiritual science, although I couldn't see what was scientific about it. As far as I could make out it was a combination of Buddhism, Christianity and eastern and western philosophy. One of its most important principles was reincarnation and karma. Mireya, though, inserted her own ideas ("research" she called it) about the indigenous people of the area in which we were now living. They were called the Comechingones, and there are none of them left, although artifacts abound, along with names of streets and, especially, inns. The main drag (a dirt road) of the village in which we lived is called *Intiuán*. But that's all new age fluff; no one really cares about the Comechingones — except her. She was convinced that she was one of them in a previous incarnation. Now that may sound absurd, but in reality, she was one of the most practical and realistic people I'd ever known. And she'd studied all there is about the Comechingones, in the Spanish conquistadors' documents. She meditated and claimed she had confirmed her previous incarnation as a spiritual fact. That was all right with me, it neither upset me nor made me jump for joy. Who was I to judge?

One warm night when we were wrapped in each other's

arms under the stars, she confided two things to me. The first was that if she hadn't been ill and with a short life expectancy, she'd never have become my lover — at least not so soon. The second was that I had been with her during that previous incarnation as a Comechingón. That was a bit much for me to chew on, but I all I said was, jokingly, "Ah, I thought you looked familiar." She laughed, poked me in the chest with her elbow and rejoined, "You're still a materialist, but you'll see." I kissed her, and she agreed that *now* was more important — at least for the evening.

She was a great studier, not only of anthroposophy but also of languages. She knew some English, German, Russian, even Chinese, but couldn't really speak any of them. She would often ask me to explain English expressions. One evening, having read and been enchanted by Poe's *The Raven,* she said, "The meaning of the word 'nevermore' is obvious: *nunca más.*" She was referring to the title of the book written by the presidential panel which investigated the crimes against humanity perpetrated by the Argentine military junta during the seventies and early eighties. "Has it been translated into English? Is the title *Nevermore?*" I told her that I didn't know if it had been translated, but if so they probably used 'Never Again', because 'nevermore' sounds too poetic. "But it's a beautiful word," she protested. "And what is the opposite, the antonym?"

I thought a moment, then said, "evermore".

"Ah, how lovely! I love that word, evermore, evermore, evermore! What would it be in Spanish? *Para siempre?* No, too pedestrian. Let's see what the dictionary says." She rushed into her study and, after a few moments, called out: "*eternamente!*" She came back clutching the dictionary.

"Evermore means *eternamente,* that's us, *mi amor.*" And she kissed me on the lips.

*

I didn't have anything to do with the school at first, except to pick her up after class. It was only two kilometers from the school to home, but mostly uphill, and I didn't want her to overexert herself. Gradually I got involved though. First one of the teachers had the idea that the school should have a magazine and they asked me to organize and edit it, or rather Mireya asked me for them, and it was of course she who told them that I knew how to do it. I asked them for pictures and written material. They gave me some pictures, but little usable text. I didn't want it to be full of Rudolf Steiner quotes, so I read up on the educational method and wrote the text myself. Then they wanted me to be on the Board of Directors. I refused that but found myself involved in a number of projects anyway, to the extent that the locals began to think of me as one of "them", the school people. And in a way I was, having become convinced that the educational method was superior to anything I'd ever seen, and that it must be heaven for the kids, compared to the hell of my own schooling.

I finished my book at the end of the year allocated to me and sent it to the foundation which had financed it. They liked it and sent it to a publisher who also liked it and sent me a one-way ticket to New York in order to sign a contract and talk over its contents. I exchanged it for a round-trip ticket, which was cheaper than the one-way according to inscrutable airline logic. It was just at that time Mireya was due to go to Buenos Aires for a hospital checkup, so everything seemed to fit in. What she hadn't told me though was that she had been feeling poorly lately. At the hospital in Buenos Aires, they told her that the nodules in her left lung had grown. She had already had an operation on her right one, and it was half its normal size, and she needed to have another operation. So, while I was being wined and dined by editors and a new agent, they were operating on her in the German hospital in Buenos Aires. She survived the operation, in fact it was successful, but she never left the hospital; they found a brain tumor, inoperable, and that combined with weakness from the operation was too much for her heart and she died a few days later.

I had been calling home with no answer, when she should have been back, so I began to worry and called a neighbor who told me the news. Mireya had been cremated by then and her ashes were in her family's plot in Buenos Aires.

I finished my business in the U.S. and went back to Villa de las Rosas, where everyone was most sympathetic. I stayed home and drank and walked farther up the Sierra than I'd ever gone, hoping to get lost for good. Royalties started to come in from the book, not in the Harry Potter league, but sufficient to last me quite a while without working. My agent was on me to write another book, but I had neither the desire nor the will to do so. I told him I'd translate the published one into Spanish. He said they could get a translator for that, but I insisted on doing it myself; it would keep me busy without having to think creatively. And it did. Gradually I came back to life and even agreed to be on the school's Board. Mireya would want that.

The original schoolhouse is an old, sturdy rancho made of adobe which, according to Sebastián, the local caretaker, was haunted by a "boy-in-white". Nobody took Sebastián seriously because nobody except him had ever seen such a boy. We humored him though and grinned among us when he wasn't around. The rest of the school — small, detached buildings housing two classrooms each — had been built around the original one. Now it was mostly used as an office. At a meeting on a day when the secretary was home sick, we would need some papers, the whereabouts of which only she knew. We didn't want to bother her, so I went to the office on that day mentioned at the beginning to look for them.

I was sitting at the desk going through a thick file of unorganized papers when a cloud opened, and a stream of light came through the window in front of me illuminating the dust particles in the air. I looked up through the window and saw a figure in white pass quickly across my view. Naturally I thought immediately of Sebastián's ghostly boy-in-white and sat there trying to decide whether to look outside or leave well enough alone. Finally, I shrugged off my fear of the unknown and stepped outside the door. An Indian girl stood next to the clay oven watching me. I knew it was Mireya, though her face was different, more indigenous-looking, darker, with higher cheek bones, more slanted eyes, somewhat shorter, older (I remembered reading that in the spiritual world everyone is 33), still beautiful. She seemed to be waiting for recognition, so when I whispered her name in a language I didn't know she smiled and approached me slowly and with her left hand extended. She spoke in the language of the Comechingones, which I understood, saying, "Will you come with me?" I replied affirmatively in the same language, although I really only thought it. I extended my right hand and just as she was about to touch it the cloud closed, the stream of light disappeared, she withdrew her hand, and I fainted.

When I didn't return to the meeting one of the teachers drove to the school to find out what happened. She found me sitting up, having just regained consciousness. She insisted that we go to Doctor Luna's house in her car, leaving mine at the school. The doctor examined me and found nothing wrong, he thought my fainting was caused by a sudden drop in blood pressure, which was now normal. The teacher drove me home and told me to rest, that she would call in the morning to see how I was. I went to bed and slept through till this morning. When I went into the bathroom to shower and looked in the mirror, I saw the face of a very old man staring back at me. Hair and beard white, wrinkles and all. As I looked, I could see myself growing older by the minute. I was very tired, and my bones ached, so I made my way, haltingly and with difficulty, back to bed. The cloud closed too quickly, I thought. If it hadn't, I would be with her now. But soon, very soon, I would die of old age, and it would be accomplished. I must have fallen asleep again (old people do that), for I was woken by an insistent telephone. It was the teacher: "Are you all right? You took a long time to answer."

"I'm fine," I said, although I didn't quite believe it yet.

"Are you sure?"

"Yes, thank you."

I replaced the receiver and walked quickly and painlessly into the bathroom. My old, original forty-two-year-old face watched me from the mirror with what looked like bemusement. "No, Mireya," I said to the other face in the mirror behind mine, "it's not time. But what's a few years, decades even, compared to *evermore*?"

The Book

I met Dr. Hableben during a working vacation in the *Traslasierra*, which means, literally, beyond-the-mountains. The mountain range in question is just east of the Andes and about five hundred miles west of Buenos Aires. So much for geography. I include it in order to indicate that my encounter with "el doctor", as he was called there, took place in a relatively remote part of the planet.

I went to the Traslasierra at the invitation of a group of families who had fled the urban chaos of Buenos Aires and wanted to start an alternative school for their children. They felt that I, as an expert of sorts in Waldorf or Steiner education and coordinator of a teacher training seminar in Buenos Aires, could provide some of the knowledge and impetus they would need.

During the course I gave and in various meetings with the aspiring school founders, I learned that the suggestion to found our kind of school came from "el doctor," and that he was keen to meet me. In fact, he invited me, in writing, to lunch with him at his house when I was finished with the group. His letter was formal, written in a spidery hand, and in German. I don't know how he knew that I speak German and I never asked him.

He lived with his housekeeper in a modest adobe house at an altitude of over five thousand feet. It took us, an Indio driver and me, three hours to reach it in a four-wheel drive pick-up mounted high over its chassis in order to navigate the three streams we had to cross. Dr. Hableben was tall, thin and wiry — and very old. His penetrating, wide-spread, once clear blue eyes were watery with age. We ate a vegetarian lunch under a canopy of grapevines lush with fruit and washed it down with limpid water from the stream that rushed by a few yards from us.

The housekeeper, an attractive young woman of obvious Indian descent, prepared the lunch and ate with us. She sat next to him, watching his every move and listening intently, although he spoke in German. Occasionally he absent-mindedly stroked her hand and looked at her in what I can only describe as a loving way.

I had expected that he would want to know how my course went and what I thought of the possibility of founding a Waldorf school in the Traslasierra valley, but he never even mentioned it. Instead, he spoke of the book he had been working on for the past twenty years. He came directly to the point. He had tried to interest some publishers in Germany, but the few who answered did so with form letters — rejection slips, of which I have also had ample experience. He wanted me to translate the book into English, my native tongue, and get it published in America.

I knew that finding a publisher for an unknown author may not be the most difficult thing in the world, but it is high on the list. I said as much. He smiled and said that it didn't matter, that the attempt, which is the important thing, must be made. He asked Mireya, in Spanish, to fetch the manuscript. She went inside the house and came back out carrying an enormous pile of papers, which she set on the table after clearing it of ants and blowing away some grape leaves. She put a stone on top of the pile, so it wouldn't blow away and resumed her seat. El doctor invited me with a gesture of his hand to look at the manuscript.

The first yellowed pages were written in small but firm letters of the old Gothic script, which didn't disappear from Germany until after the Second World War. When I lived in Germany I had made myself familiar with this oddity out of curiosity, so I could read it, but with some difficulty. I deciphered the first page, which was enough to show me that the author possessed learning, which he expressed in a philosophical style reminiscent of the nineteenth century. I leafed through the rest and noticed that towards the end the writing became spidery and shaky.

"No publisher nowadays will agree to read a handwritten manuscript," I said, trying to worm my way out of the situation. "It would have to be typed."

"Of course," the doctor said, "but when you translate it you'll type it anyway. I assume you have a word processor."

"Well, yes, but you see, I have very little time."

"Time is not important."

"To me it is," I smiled.

"Take as long as you need."

"It would take years."

"Then take them."

I sighed. "What's it about?"

"Why life, of course."

"Life?"

"UFO life, to be more specific."

I smiled, skeptically, I fear.

"I had also been skeptical about the so-called Unidentified Flying Objects because, as a scientist, I knew, firstly, that there is no human life in our solar system and, secondly, that no civilized beings can overcome the barrier of the speed of light in order to reach our system — until I read Professor Jung's treatise on the subject." He stopped, popped a dark blue grape into his mouth and kissed Mireya's hand, which must have been sweeter than the grape, to judge by his expression.

"Go on, please," I said. Many years previously I had read Carl Jung's little book on flying saucers but had only a vague recollection of it.

"Jung opines that UFO's must exist because so many people have seen them down through the centuries. What he doubts is that they exist physically."

"Then they are imagined?"

"Not at all. He meant that they exist psychically. And psychic phenomena were very real to him, as they are to me." He leaned toward me and held his hand in front of my eyes. "This hand is physically real, is it not?"

"As far as I'm concerned it is, though some philosophers might not agree."

"And it also exists psychically," he continued, ignoring the philosophers. "Somewhere, the psychic equivalent of my hand exists as an idea, but ideas are also real. If such is the case, and I assure you that it is, then psychic phenomena may have their physical equivalence in another place in the cosmos. Do you follow me?"

"I think so, yes."

"My hypothesis was that it might be possible to so train the psyche, or the mind if you prefer, so that we could find and witness the physical equivalents of the UFOs."

"Do you mean, Herr Doktor, that some interstellar intelligence has been psychically projecting what we call UFOs, and that they really exist, I mean physically, somewhere else?"

"Exactly. So I decided to dedicate myself to finding the 'somewhere else'. The book is a faithful account of my experiments — successful ones, I might add — and their results."

I know it sounds nutty, but the doctor didn't come across as a nut. "Could you tell me something about those results?"

"Yes, but first the method. I spent years perfecting a technique of concentration and meditation which finally enabled me to leave my body at night during sleep and make my way to the planet whose inhabitants have been sending us their psychic images for ages."

"Wouldn't an obvious objection be that you were dreaming?" I asked, almost apologetically.

"A special kind of conscious dreaming," he said, as though that explained it. "Of course, I didn't do it alone. I reached the world of spiritual ideas, a place where few earthlings have been, and transmitted my request to proceed to that planet. I had no idea where it was in the physical universe, you see."

"To whom did you transmit the request?"

"To a council of spiritual beings. They decided in my favor and assigned one of their number to guide me. If you must know — it isn't in the book, you see — it was an angel, perhaps my own, he didn't say."

He popped another grape, so I did the same.

"He took me by the hand, psychically, that is, and we were there in no time."

"What was it called?" I asked with a straight face, "the planet I mean."

"It took me some time to learn the language, although it wasn't much different from some of our own. The best translation I can make is ... Earth."

We both smiled. I glanced at Mireya, who smiled along with us.

"And what kind of people — I mean beings, inhabited it?"

"You were right the first time, people, like us. The only intelligent beings in the universe are human beings."

I found later in studying The Book that this was only an assumption on his part. He had not, after all, investigated the entire universe.

"The beginning was difficult, first of all because I was only there psychically and was therefore invisible to the inhabitants. Furthermore, I had made no provision for the care of my body back on Earth — our Earth, that is — so I had to return before I starved to death or dehydrated."

"But before you came back what observations did you make?"

"Few, there was so little time and so many overwhelming impressions. As you will have guessed, they are very advanced technologically. And their airships are indeed what we call UFOs, of many shapes and sizes. I was like an aboriginal suddenly transported to a metropolis and didn't understand half the things I was seeing. I also had the impression, however, that they were deeply troubled. That's all, though. I had to go."

"How did you do that? Was the angel still with you?"

"No, he had deposited me there, wished me good luck and left."

"So how then?"

"You must understand that the difficulty is not in returning but getting there and staying. The whole time one must exert a great force of will. The moment it is relaxed you are whisked back to your body. This control of the will is something you develop through meditation — a powerful mixture of will and thought, or, I should say, thinking raised to the level of pure will. So all I had to do was relax my will and I was back in bed."

"Here, in the Traslasierra?"

"Yes, of course. Such things are only possible in places of great peace. I was extremely hungry and thirsty, for I had been gone for three days. I won't bore you with details now, it's all in the book anyway. After a certain amount of effort, I found someone trustworthy who had medical experience and was willing to stay here with my body and control the intravenous serum and feeding."

"And you went back?"

"Yes, it was easier the second time, and not so traumatic."

"Did you find out why the people there are troubled?"

"Yes, I did. They are so computerized and comfortable that they have forgotten the meaning of life. They are spiritually empty."

"No religion?"

"Plenty of religions. But only fanatics and simpletons believe in them."

"And what about the ones who send the UFOs here?"

"Naturally I wondered about them and decided to seek them out. I found them after many false starts and after having surmounted many barriers. It's all in the book."

"Yes, of course, but who are they?"

"They are a group of individuals who have maintained a long tradition of esoteric knowledge. But they must keep their activities secret because, you see, a kind of self-imposed autocratic state has been established in order to control the total anarchy that reigned until about a millennium ago. They are a kind of occult brotherhood — or sisterhood rather — there being are more women than men in it." He glanced meaningfully at Mireya, who smiled at him as though she understood what he was saying in German, which seemed unlikely to me. "They long ago discovered essentially the same meditation technique I used and had found us, another human race, just as I found them. It is they and their forerunners who have been sending signs to us in the form of Unidentified Flying Objects all this time."

"UFOs are really spaceships then?" I asked.

"On the Other Earth, yes," he answered patiently. "Here they are manifestations of light — round, oblong, flat, spherical — transmitted psychically to us by a complex process of projective heliography. All the rest — little green men, abductions — are figments or outright fabrications."

"But what are they trying to say by these signs?"

"That we are not alone. They are meant as encouragement to attempt contact. Once contact is made, they want to warn us not to fall into the same error their civilization has."

"Too much technology?"

"Technology is inevitable, but the human spirit must not be neglected as a result."

"But why aren't they more clear, I mean just come out and say what they mean instead of signs that no one understands?"

"It's all in the book."

"Yes, but ..."

"Light is the only sensible element in which they can manifest themselves at such distances; it is somewhere between the physical and the spiritual. Otherwise, it is only possible to communicate in the spiritual state and for that — well, it takes two to tango." The last five words, his "joke", he said in English.

"You mean that they can only communicate with someone who has mastered the meditation technique?"

"That is correct."

"And are you the only ... er ... earthling with whom they can communicate?"

"Directly, yes, as far as I know. Indirectly they are communicating with us all via the signs."

"Herr Doktor," I began as respectfully as I could, "forgive my asking, but do you have any proof of all this?" I was leading up to saying what I was thinking, that even if I believed him, and I wasn't sure that I did, it would be mostly due to his most convincing presence. Someone reading his Gothic prose would be much less inclined to give him the benefit of the doubt. But his reply, which he shot out with no hesitation, surprised me.

"Yes, I do."

I waited, not wanting to sound like a prosecuting attorney, or even an editor.

Doctor Hableben turned to his companion and took her hand.

"Mireya" — he looked at the girl, smiling — "is from that Other Earth."

"But ... but how ...?" I stammered.

"Wait, I'll explain. It's all in the book in great detail, but I'll try to explain in synthesis. She was one of the group who sent the signs and we communicated on a spiritual plane. She was my contact person with her group. We could have had no karmic history, having come from different worlds. Nevertheless we ... well, yes, we fell in love is the only expression you will understand."

"It is a lovely expression," Mireya said in perfect German, surprising me again, for I had fallen into the trap of believing her to be the doctor's primitive and docile lover/house-keeper.

"But how did she —" I stopped and, embarrassed, directed my question to Mireya. "How did you get here?"

"I incarnated in a self-less body."

"A *what* body?"

"Sí," she continued in Spanish. "It is not frequent, but some bodies are born without selfs. Many of them die, but not all. You see, due to the population explosion there simply aren't enough selfs, or egos, if you prefer the Greek, to go around anymore."

I was literally speechless, if not selfless.

The doctor continued. "At birth, here in the Traslasierra. It was all arranged beforehand. She was born to a young unmarried girl whom I befriended — I knew the baby would be Mireya of course — and took responsibility for her education and upbringing".

Mireya laughed. "So, you see I'm really quite a bit older than I look. I was almost fifty in the Other Earth, add thirty here and —"

"Eighty," I said, stupidly.

"Yes," Doctor Hableben said. "And I will be a hundred this year, which means I won't be around much longer. So Mireya —"

"Excuse me, Herr Doktor, a question."

"No," he said, reading my mind, "I no longer go to the Other Earth. My powers of concentration and will have deteriorated with old age. In fact, I must now terminate this conversation in order to rest. Please forgive me."

"Oh no, please rest, Herr Doktor."

"It may be a final rest. In any case, it would serve no purpose to continue. Will you take the manuscript now into your care and translate it into English?"

"May I ask —?"

"Why you?"

"Yes, why me?"

"As I said, Mireya and I had no mutual karma; ours is the first karmic relationship between beings of our two worlds. But you and I, my young friend, have a complex karmic history going back many lives. You were destined to be here today and receive the opportunity to do as I ask. You are free, however, to decide."

That explanation, his penetrating eyes, and what he said about going to his final rest, were convincing. Nevertheless, I took a minute to make sure that the decision would be my own. I walked a few yards away from the table and gazed down into the valley of the Traslasierra, a still idyllic part of our poor deteriorating world, not the Other, but our own, Earth. Then I went back and stood before him.

Ja, Herr Doktor. Ich will.

"Thank you. Now I must retire." He rose with difficulty and took my hand. "Please stay in contact with Mireya." He walked to the door of the house, where he had to stoop to enter. Mireya called the driver and put the manuscript in a strong shopping bag and handed it to me. We kissed on the right cheeks, as is the custom, and she followed Doctor Hableben into the house.

Enclosed please find the first three chapters of the doctor's book. I calculate that the translation work will take me an-other year. There are over a thousand pages of small writing. I would be grateful if you could advise me if you are interested in this book, which may well be the most important one since the Bible. If you are not, please return the manuscript in the enclosed self-addressed, stamped envelope. Thank you.

Yours sincerely,

Frank Thomas Smith

PS. I am doing my best to simplify the author's style with-out affecting the content.

His legal heir, Ms. Mireya Galvez, approves.

by Roberto Fox

The Redheaded Pizza

Romano, the redheaded pizza-parlor man, has already made at least a hundred pizzas this afternoon. Customers love his pizzas because of the technique he learned in Italy and his artistic touches. He had also learned to only use bio-dynamic ingredients according to the agricultural method founded by Rudolf Steiner. In Romano's opinion, a well-made pizza, with healthy bio-dynamic ingredients, is a living work of art. But today he has so much work that he makes one pizza after another almost automatically: cheese, napolitana, onion, salami etc., large, small and medium.

"One large cheese!" the waiter calls.

"Always the same," Romano sighs.

When he finishes shaping the dough and putting on the cheese and tomato sauce, he stops a moment, smiles, and instead of putting the olives any which way, he carefully places two of them at the same height. Then he puts another a bit lower between the first two. He cuts a piece of red pepper and places it below the third olive forming a smile on the face he has drawn on the pizza. Finally, he puts on two pieces of red pepper for the ears and a generous spoonful of tomato sauce over the forehead. He observes his work, laughs out loud and says, "Welcome, redheaded pizza," and places it in the oven with the long-handled, wooden shovel that pizza-makers use.

When the pizza is done, he takes it out of the oven and sees that it looks more than ever like a human face because the oven's heat has given it a lively color.

"I won't sell it," he says to himself. "It's too pretty. Maybe I'll eat it myself when we close." And he places it on the top of the oven to keep it warm.

The redheaded pizza hears what Romano says and is proud of his creator's praise. She is impatient for closing time.

At about one-thirty, when the pizza-parlor is full of customers, a fat man complains in a loud voice to the waiter: "Where's my pizza? I ordered it an hour ago!"

The waiter knows that the fat man didn't order the pizza an hour ago, but it could well have been a half-hour. Therefore, he rushes to the counter to see what happened to the order. He sees the redheaded pizza and thinks it's the fat man's. And if not, it doesn't matter, because if it's another customer's, Romano, who is very busy preparing new pizzas, can make another. The waiter takes the redheaded pizza, puts it on his tray and goes to the fat man's table.

The redheaded pizza was dozing when the waiter removed her from her warm spot on the oven. When she realizes that she is being carried through the air on a tray away from Romano, she has a fright. And imagine her terror when she is placed in front of the fat man who looks at her with little pig's eyes, licks his lips and picks up knife and fork ready to cut.

With a great effort, the redheaded pizza jumps off the plate before the waiter's bulging eyes and rolls to the edge of the table, hesitates a moment at seeing the floor so far below, decides to risk it and rolls over the edge, landing on the floor without damage.

"What happened?" the fat man cries, looking at his empty plate.

"Stop!" the waiter yells at the pizza, who is rolling away from the table. "Come back here this minute!"

But the redheaded pizza, on seeing that the path to Romano is blocked by the waiter, decides to go out onto the street. The fat man runs after her shouting, "Stop! Stop! I want to eat you."

"You'll never eat me, Fatso," the redheaded pizza answers. The only one who can eat me is my creator, Romano.

She passes a German shepherd who wakes up with a start upon smelling her pass. "Bow-wo-wow!" he barks, meaning: "Stop! Stop! I want to eat you."

"You'll never eat me, you mangy mutt," the redheaded pizza answers. "The only one who can eat me is my creator, Romano."

Nevertheless, the German shepherd runs behind the pizza barking: "Bow-wo-wow!"

The redheaded pizza crosses the street against a red light causing several cars to brake suddenly. A policeman, who is resting in a café drinking coffee and reading a newspaper, hears the screech of brakes and steps out of the café to see what's happening. When he sees the redheaded pizza, the fat man and the German shepherd crossing the street against the red light, he takes out his whistle and blows until his face is blue.

"Stop!" he yells. "It's forbidden to cross the street when the light is red!"

The redheaded pizza reaches the other side of the street and continues rolling between the people's legs. The policeman realizes that he's hungry and that the pizza would be a good excuse to return to the police station an hour early and share it with his buddies.

"Stop!" he shouts, "I want to eat you in the police station."

But the redheaded pizza keeps rolling on and answers the policeman: "The cops will never eat me. The only one who can eat me is my creator, Romano."

And she rolls on and on down the street followed by the fat man, the dog and the policeman, until she arrives at the outskirts of town. There she almost crashes into a redheaded girl who is fixing a flat tire on her bicycle.

"Hi, delicious redheaded pizza," the girl says. "Why are you rolling down the street like that? You're going to get cold."

The redheaded pizza looks back and sees that the fat man, the dog and the policeman are getting closer. "Will you help me?" she asks the girl.

"Of course," the girl answers. "What's wrong?"

"You've got to hide me, or the fat man, the dog and the policeman will eat me."

"Poor pizza," the girl says. "Wait, let me think." She puts a finger on her nose, as she always does when trying to solve a problem. "I know," she exclaims. "Quick, get beneath my bike as though you were a wheel."

The redheaded pizza rolls below the front end of the bike, and the girl tightens a nut till she is firmly attached.

"Did you see a redheaded pizza pass through here?" the fat man, puffing, asks the girl.

"Where is the redheaded pizza?" the policeman yells between blasts on his whistle.

"Bow-wo-wow," the German shepherd barks with its tongue hanging out.

"She went that way," the girl says, pointing to the woods.

The fat man, the dog and the policeman run into the woods, each one hoping to catch the redheaded pizza and eat her by himself.

"I think you're safe now," the girls says. "But you can't stay here because they might come back."

"I want to return to the pizza parlor where I was born," the redheaded pizza says. "The problem is that every person or animal I meet wants to eat me." And looking up at the girl's pretty face, asks: "Do you want to eat me, too?"

"To tell the truth, I do," the girl admits. "You look delicious and I'm hungry. But if you don't want me to eat you, I won't."

"Look," the redheaded pizza says thankfully, "you're my friend, so you can eat me with my creator, Romano."

"Oh!" the girl cries, "How lucky I am:"

"Yes," the redheaded pizza agrees, "but how are we going to get to the pizza parlor of my birth?"

"On my bike, of course. Is it far?"

"Pretty far. But let's go!"

The girl sits on the bike and pedals down the street with the redheaded pizza acting as the front wheel. Several times the redheaded pizza thinks she's going to break, but with a great act of will she keeps firm until they reach the pizza parlor. The door is closed because all the lunch customers have left. It is three o'clock in the afternoon.

The girl gets off the bike and knocks on the door. Within, Romano has just discovered that his redheaded pizza isn't in the oven and he asks the waiter what happened. When he realizes that the pizza has escaped in order to avoid being eaten by the fat man, he is sad. It had never been his intention to let anyone but himself eat the redheaded pizza.

He walks slowly to the door against which someone is knocking. He is surprised to see the girl outside and thinks, "I have never seen such a pretty girl before."

"Are you the pizza-maker?" she asks, also surprised. She hadn't expected to meet such a handsome young man with eyes so intense that they seem to penetrate her like forks.

"Yes," he confirms. "I'm Romano."

"Romano?"

"And you? What is your name?"

"I am Romana."

"Romana?"

"Romana y Romano," she says. "How funny!"

Romana unscrews the redheaded pizza from her bicycle and gives it to Romano, who receives it joyfully. "My dear redheaded pizza!" he cries.

On seeing her creator with her olive-eyes, the redheaded pizza smiles with her pepper-mouth and says: "At last I'm home."

Romano puts the redheaded pizza in the oven to heat up. When it's ready, he takes it out with the long wooden shovel, and he and Romana eat it with so much relish that they fall in love in the act. They marry shortly afterwards and have a family of seven children — four girls and three boys, all redheads. They always remember the redheaded pizza and they tell their children the story of how they met because of her.

They also tell them how delicious she was.

by Roberto Fox

To Hunt a Nazi

Time past and time future
What might have been and what has been
Point to one end, which is always present.

T.S. Eliot

There are moments in the present, but also in the past and I hope in the future, when I have the urge to pull Eliot out from my bookcase and read Four Quartets. The moments are usually when I'm bogged down with a story or a poem and think that a solution simply isn't possible. Somehow Quartets — only that, not other poems by Eliot or any other poet — inspires me or at least gives me hope that anything is possible.

I was meditating on these three lines when the phone rang. I was sitting at my desk with my back to my picture window overlooking the Buenos Aires municipal golf course in Palermo Park. I can't face the park while working because its beauty distracts me. Anyway, it was foggy, a common occurrence on autumn mornings, though the sun usually burns the fog away by mid-morning. I picked up the phone and swiveled around towards the park: "Hola"

"Mr. Roberto Fox, please?" a woman's voice asked in English.

"Speaking."

"One moment please, Mr. Fox, I'll connect you to Ms. Gutiérrez." Obviously, an executive type too busy to dial her own numbers. Strike one. After a minute of *The Four Seasons*, I was about to hang up when ... "Mr. Fox?"

"Yes, I already said so."

"I'm so sorry to keep you waiting; another call, very urgent, came just as we were trying to get you."

"That's okay," I lied, "what can I do for you?"

"I'm Andrea Gutiérrez of the Simon Wiesenthal Foundation in Vienna." She waited for me to react, but I didn't. "Do you know about us, Mr. Fox?" She had a slight Spanish accent.

"Yes, you hunt Nazis. As far as I know Mr. Wiesenthal gave Mossad the tip that led to the capture of Eichmann in Buenos Aires in ... when was it?"

"1963. Yes, you are informed."

"Not really. I read The House on Garibaldi Street about the operation."

"It's very informative."

"Again, what can I do for you, Ms. Gutiérrez?"

"I'll be in Buenos Aires on Wednesday ..." (it was Sunday) "... and I'd like to speak with you when I'm there."

"What about?"

"About the possibility of you helping us ... but I'd rather not go into details on the phone, if you don't mind."

"I don't mind, except I'd like to know how you got my name and why you think I can or should help you."

"Osvaldo Romberg gave me your name."

"Osvaldo?" I said, becoming intrigued. He'd worked as an undercover agent for me back during my spook days. "I haven't seen him in decades. Where is he now?"

"Israel, he's a well-known artist there." Her voice was getting lower and her sentences shorter, so it was obvious that she wasn't thrilled about giving any information over the phone. "Will you have some time for me on Wednesday, Mr. Fox?"

"Okay. What time?"

"Five-ish?"

"No ishes, please."

"Five then."

"Where?"

"Your apartment?"

"All right. It's La Pampa ..."

"I know where it is."

"Uh huh. And what else do you know about me?"

"I'll tell you on Wednesday. Thank you." (click)

I'd almost forgotten about Andrea Gutiérrez by Wednesday morning when I opened my appointments book and saw her name. I frowned, shrugged, laced up my running shoes, and took the squeaky elevator down the four floors to the exit, which opens right into the park. I started my leisurely jog around the lake in brilliant autumn sunshine, waving to the ducks who seemed annoyed that I had no tidbits to give them. At least fifteen girls in shorts, jiggling tits and ponytails overtook me like fillies passing an old dray horse — some twice. I was used to it.

I almost knocked down our portero when I pulled up at the entrance to my apartment building. "Buen dia, Don Roberto," he said, exuding the odor of last night's wine and garlic. "Still running, I see." He thought I was mad for wasting all that energy for nothing.

"Buen dia, Julio," I answered. "Yes, and someday I'll get where I'm going." He laughed, more convinced than ever of my insanity.

I checked the web and found that the Wiesenthal Foundation had an office in Buenos Aires, so why the hell were they calling me from Vienna — and why were they calling me at all? Forget it and concentrate on your work, I told myself. Reading Four Quartets the day before had gotten me over a bump in imagination, and I was sailing through the pages of my book. After a few hours I called it a day (I'm no workaholic) and walked over to an Italian restaurant on Avenida Libertador, where I indulged in a delicious dish of mostacholes and a small bottle of Santa Julia Malbec red wine. Then I strolled back home and read some Dostoyevsky in bed as preparation for my daily siesta. I remembered Ms. Gutiérrez though and set the alarm for 4:30.

At six o'clock I was still reading Dostoyevsky and sipping mate tea through a bronze straw when the phone rang. "The airport was fogged in," Andrea Gutiérrez said rapidly without identifying herself. "We were diverted to Sao Paulo, then there was a mechanical problem. I just arrived. I'm in the airport I can be at your place in a half hour."

"Forty-five minutes would be more like it," I said, "but you must be exhausted."

"I am, but I must see you today."

"Okay, I'll be waiting."

It was worth the wait. She was certainly exhausted, but she'd obviously done the best she could in the airport ladies' room before taking a taxi for the long drive to the city. She was about thirty, maybe a bit more, had long black hair parted in the middle, large black almost unblinking eyes, very thin with no breasts to speak of, and quite beautiful in a Latin way, which is my favorite way.

"Máte?" I asked, offering her the gourd.

She frowned. "I could really use a cup of coffee, Mr. Fox."

"It's instant," I warned, "but good instant. Milk? And let's drop the formalities; I'm Roberto."

"I thought you were American."

"Right, but everyone calls me Roberto here."

"Oh, like in For Whom the Bell Tolls?"

"Something like that, but I don't wear a hat."

"Black, please, one sugar."

The fog had cleared by midday, so I could watch the golfers from the kitchen window while waiting for the water to boil. I promised myself for the umpteenth time to take up the game someday.

"So, Andrea, I ask you once more: What can I do for you?"

She lifted her attaché case onto her lap, clicked the fasteners but didn't open it. "We'd like you to find someone for us."

I lifted my eyebrows as though surprised. "Some Nazi?"

"Yes, his name is Walter Kutschmann."

"And why do you want me, of all people, to find him?"

She crossed her legs, shapely ones by the way, and flipped up the attaché lid. "Osvaldo Romberg told me you were an airline investigator and are now a private detective."

"As I already told you, Andrea, I haven't seen Osvaldo in a dog's age, so he's not up to date. It's true that I was an investigator for the International Air Transport Association and that I was a private detective. But now I'm neither." I smiled, if you can call what my face does a smile. "Sorry to disappoint you."

"Oh? Are you retired then?"

"I took early retirement from IATA, saved something of the detective income, and along with the pittance I earn as an author, I get by quite well here because of the favorable exchange rate."

"I see, but ..."

"Hold on. You're getting my whole bio, and I don't know anything about you." she didn't like that, I could tell.

"What would you like to know?" she said.

"Are you Jewish?"

"Yes."

"Are you using your real name?"

She didn't answer right away, probably deciding whether to act offended or not. Finally, she smiled. "Why do you ask that?" as though it were a ridiculous question.

"Gutiérrez is a fairly common name around here, I know a half dozen, and none of them are Jews. Are you Israeli?"

"Yes, and my name is Sara Romberg. Satisfied?"

"Ah — related to Osvaldo?"

"Cousins."

"Wonderful. Why the phony name then? Wait, let me guess: Mossad."

"Wrong. Simon Wiesenthal Foundation."

"One doesn't necessarily preclude the other."

"Yes, it does," she said. "We stay as far away from Mossad as possible."

"In order to stay out of trouble?"

"Yes, and for public relations reasons, especially since Eichmann. Also, Mossad has other priorities now."

"That I can believe — like Palestine, Iran, not to mention Washington. Sorry, I couldn't resist the Washington bit."

"Why? It's true. We must remain above suspicion. When we find out where a Nazi is we notify Germany first, then the country where his crimes took place, which could be Germany, Poland, Russia, France, etcetera."

"What about the country he's in?"

"Depends on the country and if there's already a warrant out for his arrest."

"Argentina?"

"Depends. Look Roberto, can we get to the point?"

Now it was my turn to smile, inwardly at least. I was no longer controlling the conversation, which was unusual, but what the hell, I like change. "Sure, shoot."

She sighed histrionically. "Thanks. Are you willing to

help?"

"Good question. Now here's mine: Why should I?"

"We'll pay you of course." This was getting serious.

"Do you know T.S. Eliot, Sara?"

She frowned. "Some."

"Four Quartets?"

"April is the cruelest month."

"Right, very good. It's April, when I'm especially susceptible to cruelty, so ..."

"What could be crueler than the holocaust?"

"Good point. What did this guy ... Kutch ... what?"

"Kutschmann, Walter Kutschmann."

"What did he do?"

She finally opened the attaché-case and took a file out, then closed the case and placed it on the table. "Gestapo SS-Untersturmführer Dr. Walter Kutschmann," she read from the file, "responsible for the murder of twenty Polish professors and their families in Lemberg in 1941, as well as having participated in the murder of several thousand Jewish inhabitants of the cities of Brzezny and Podhajce ..." She handed me two sheets of paper. "Here's his biography."

"Nice guy," I said after having read it. "He deserted to Spain in 1944. How do you know he's in Argentina?"

"Mr. Wiesenthal found out. I think he just guessed, because as you must know Argentina is a favorite postwar Nazi destination. He checked with a source in Rome, who advised him that Kutschmann obtained a Vatican passport and an Argentine visa in 1946, both under a false name."

"What name?"

"That would make it too easy," she said wryly. "We don't know."

"How do you know the source is reliable then?"

"She always has been. You mentioned Eichmann."

"But that was a Mossad operation."

"Our source is well connected to the German community in Spain and used to give the information to Mossad when they were still interested. As I already told you, they aren't any more. So she came to us."

"So what she knows is hearsay."

"Very reliable hearsay, yes."

"Together with Wiesenthal's intuition."

She stared at me for a good minute, then said, "Simon Wiesenthal is a great man. I'll tell you a story about him. His friend, also a former Mauthausen concentration camp inmate, related it to me. They were together at the friend's house. He had become a well-to-do jewelry manufacturer. After dinner he said, 'Simon, if you had gone back to building houses, you'd be a millionaire. Why didn't you?' 'You're a religious man,' replied Wiesenthal. 'You believe in God and life after death. I also believe. When we come to the other world and meet the millions of Jews who died in the camps and they ask us, What have you done? there will be many answers. You will say, I became a jeweler, another will say, I have smuggled coffee and American cigarettes. Another will say, I built houses. But I will say, I did not forget you.' Simon Wiesenthal has very good intuition."

I had already more or less decided to do what I could for

these good people, but a couple of things still bothered me. I said, "Okay, Sara, maybe I can help you, but I still have two questions."

"Yes?" she said, leaning forward as if I had already accomplished something.

"Why the false name if you're only representing Wiesenthal?"

She smiled, obviously relieved. "It's not false. I was born in Argentina as Andrea Gutiérrez because my father, when arriving here before the war without documents, told the immigration people his name — Georg Romberg — but the clerk didn't understand him, or didn't want to, so he wrote Jorge Gutiérrez on the entry document he gave my father. So that was our name until we emigrated to Israel, when I was a child, where we got back our identity."

I nodded, having heard stories like that before. "Are you still an Argentine citizen?"

"Yes, I have both passports. And you, Roberto? Fox could be a Jewish name."

I thought of something I hadn't thought of in decades. "There was a rumor that a great-grandfather was a Jewish money lender — a fox — in Liverpool, but my father vehemently denied it."

She laughed, flashing uneven but sexy teeth. Can teeth be sexy? "Good, then you have motivation. What else do you want to know?"

"Going back to the 'why me' question. That I was with IATA and a private investigator, and that I was recommended by Osvaldo Romberg, still doesn't seem sufficient motive for you, and Mr. Wiesenthal with his excellent intuition, to be so anxious to employ me for this particular job."

She seemed to be ready for that one, too. "You speak German, even translated a book from German to English when you lived in Germany."

"You have done your homework. Yes, Das Mikado Projekt, it became a best seller, much to everyone's surprise. But I had done the translation for a small, fixed fee, so that didn't help me much. I also wrote the screen play and acted in the German film and insisted on a share of the profits. It flopped." We both laughed.

"Anything else?" I insisted. "Speaking German is helpful, but still ..."

"There is something else," she interrupted, "the most important thing about you, Roberto."

I waited.

"You have contacts with the German community here."

"Do I?"

"The Rudolf Steiner Schule, for example."

"Oh that. But no, I have no direct contact with the school; I only know a few anthroposophists, who can hardly be called Nazis. In fact ..."

"... where a certain Jessica Kutschmann, former Hitler-Jugend group leader, teaches physical education. Do you know her?"

I was stunned. "No, I don't know any teachers at the school. She must have been very young."

"Yes, they were all mostly very young. But it's not about her."

"So you think she's related to Kutschmann. Or do you know it?"

"We're not sure, but the name is not common. And there's a resemblance."

I knew a few Germans here in Argentina because I used to live in a Buenos Aires suburb, Florida — pronounced Flor-ee-da — where many German immigrants settled during and after the war, including some Nazis and some Jews, who seemed to get along quite well there. Occasionally I would stop off in a bar-restaurant ostentatiously named "Maxim", owned and run by Heinz, a professional waiter, conscript in the German army during WWII, who had surrendered to the Americans in Italy and subsequently worked as a bartender-waiter in an NCO club, during which time he also met, impregnated and wed his Italian wife, Venusia. He considered the American army to be the best employer he ever had but was laughingly critical because they kept encouraging him to escape. He did, finally, but not to a hungry Germany-in-ruins. He stowed away on an Argentine ship. On arrival in Buenos Aires he stood in line with the crew, who had fed him during the journey and taught him the only Spanish word he knew: tripulante (crew), which got him off the ship in Buenos Aires with nary a nod from the migrations official. After working for a year as a waiter in a German restaurant, he sent for Venusia and the daughter he had never seen. Happy ending: "Maxim", where Venusia was the cook and had to learn to prepare *Eisbein mit Sauerkraut* for the German customers, despite considering it barbaric.

Eichmann, using the alias Clement, had been a customer there, according to Heinz, but he always ordered a bottle of cheap wine and a Schnitzel and sat in a corner by himself reading the Freie Presse, Buenos Aires's fascist newspaper. In my time, a couple of years later, the bar customers were mostly Germans who had prospered in Argentina as businessmen; the only exception being an alcoholic former U-boat commander. I rather liked going there to practice my rusty German, and they liked having a real-life American to berate for stupidly letting the Russians take half of Europe. I couldn't help agreeing with them, but my counterargument that they had only themselves to blame was hard to rebut.

One longtime resident was a philosopher of sorts, and we had interesting discussions about politics, religion and life in general. He was a pragmatist and called me a romantic. He went so far as to suggest that I meet up with the anthroposophists, who held similar outlandish views.

"Ah, here's one now," he exclaimed one evening. A thin elderly man, slightly stooped, had entered with a younger woman who had oriental features. The philosopher introduced them as Herr und Frau Kunst and suggested to Herr Kunst that they invite me to their table as someone who was almost as crazy as they. He said it with a big smile and the couple laughed. "We'll find out which of us is crazy on the other side," Herr Kunst retorted. The philosopher laughed, shook hands with them, said, "Indeed we will, if there is another side," tipped his hat to me and left.

"Please do join us, Herr … Sorry, I didn't get the name."

"Fox," I said, "but I don't want to intrude."

"Not at all, we are always glad to have a guest for lunch, and our philosopher friend must have had a reason for suggesting it."

Once seated, they both ordered pasta, and I followed

suit. "Frau Venusia makes excellent Italian food, which in any case is better than the German," Frau Kunst said.

"Yes," her husband agreed, "and it's because she puts her heart into it." Then, looking at me with clear blue eyes, "I detect an accent, Herr Fox. You are not German, I presume."

I told him how I had learned German when I was stationed in Germany in the U.S. army. I didn't mention my previous studies in German and Russian at the Army Language School in Monterey. Herr Kunst congratulated me, saying that few Americans learned German. "I've never been able to completely master German grammar, though," I said, "which is tortuous."

"You do very well," Frau Kunst objected. "Gunther and I are still struggling with Spanish after all these years."

Cutting off the small talk, Gunther Kunst asked me why the philosopher had initiated our meeting. "Why are you almost as crazy as we?"

"He said I should meet the anthroposophists because I'm a romantic — according to him."

"I see. So, you've never heard of Anthroposophy or Rudolf Steiner?"

I admitted my ignorance of the subject, so they invited me to participate in a study group in their home. Normally I would have begged off, but the conversation leading up to the invitation interested me. Apparently, this Steiner was an occidental initiate who coalesced the eastern philosophy of reincarnation and karma with western science and Christianity and founded a movement called Anthroposophy. I had been going to the meetings for over a year prior to Sara Romberg's arrival on the scene. That was what she called my "contacts in the German community". I would have laughed at her when she said that, for the people in my study group, despite being German, were certainly not connected with Nazis. In fact, Anthroposophy had been banned in Nazi Germany and Gunther Kunst, it turned out, was Jewish. However, ...

One of the members of the group was Wolfgang Kleinhuber, director of Osram, a large German electrical appliances company, in Argentina. One evening I asked Frau Kunst to call a taxi for me because my car was being repaired in a garage. Kleinhuber offered to drop me off at home as we were going in the same direction. On the way we stopped in a café on Avenida Libertador. Kleinhuber, knowing that I had worked for IATA, wanted to ask me a few "technical" questions.

Kleinhuber wanted to know if sales agents — passenger and cargo — received different levels of commission from the airlines depending on their production, and if such "over-commissions" were passed on to the agents' clients. Easy question, easy answer: yes. So, it is obviously beneficial for a client, especially a large company, to buy transportation from a good producing agent. Then he asked me if I knew the agency "All-Ways". I did of course and told him that they were one of the largest producers in the country.

"They're Jews, aren't they?" Kleinhuber asked matter-of-factly. I answered affirmatively in the same manner.

He studied his coffee-cup a moment, then asked, "Are they reliable?"

"As far as I know, yes. Why do you ask?"

"Well, we're thinking of changing agencies and All-Ways

has been recommended. But my sales manager is reluctant. He has a thing about Jews." He shrugged, smiling.

"I would think it would be the other way around."

"What do you mean?"

"That they'd have a thing about Germans."

The sarcasm rolled right off him. "No, I understand they give a lot of business to Lufthansa."

"Well, you're the boss," I said, "not him."

"True, but a sales manager must sell, and mine is very good." He looked down at the table as though thinking. "His sister is a teacher at the Rudolf Steiner School in Florida." Kleinhuber meant that as some kind of recommendation, I guess.

"I think I'll have a beer," I said. "How about you?" The subject was making me thirsty. We ordered a bottle of Heineken. After the first glass, Kleinhuber invited me to lunch at the German club the following week, wanted me to meet his sales manager. The German club was the last place I wanted to have lunch, but the dangling karma strings were coming together in a way which made it impossible for me to refuse.

The German Club in Buenos Aires looks like it had been transplanted directly from Prussia in the nineteenth century. When I arrived, I saw Kleinhuber leaning against the bar talking with a guy I assumed to be his Sales Manager.

"Sorry I'm late, Wolfgang," I lied, "got caught in traffic." It was only ten minutes after the agreed time, which for Argentines is early, but for Germans is late.

"Not a problem, Roberto," he smiled. "I'd like you to meet

Pedro Olmo. Pedro, Roberto Fox."

The other guy turned to face me. He was tall and well built, around sixty, obviously in shape, graying black hair brushed straight back, bushy eyebrows and a mouth cum protruding lower lip which seemed too low for his face, immaculately dressed. He bowed slightly and said, "Sehr angenehm". He may have been pleased to meet me, but his unsmiling face didn't show it. I assumed they had been talking about Kleinhuber's interest in using All-Ways as Osram's travel agency and his sales manager's aversion to the idea. And I was there to convince him.

"What will you have to drink, Roberto?" Kleinhuber asked.

"Is that sherry you're drinking?"

"Yes, excellent Spanish sherry," Pedro Olmo replied in excellent German. Pedro Olmo? So what? I told myself. Argentina has a large German-Argentine community and many second-generation Argentines speak fluent German.

I ordered the same and we engaged in small talk about the traffic and Argentina's chances to win the World Cup, then moved to our reserved table. The waiter was Argentine, so we ordered in Spanish. Pedro Olmo's accent was thicker than the steak he ordered. Having consumed his bife de lomo and quite a bit of German white wine, Olmo opened up a bit. He thought that Argentina's team was very good, but undisciplined; therefore, he was betting on Germany. He even smiled, something he did with a certain charm. I told them I liked Brazil, which shut them up. Personally, I neither like soccer nor understand it, but during many years living among fanatics I'd learned that everyone loves Brazil's imaginative soccer, whether they win or lose.

Finally, Kleinhuber came to the point. "Roberto, you know the agency All-Ways. We're thinking of changing agencies and would like to know what you think of them — if you don't mind of course."

Had he really not told Olmo of our previous conversation? I pretended to think about it, then said, "Well, I only know them professionally, but I can safely say that they have a successful business with many important clients."

"I understand that the owners are Jews," Olmo said, coming right to the point.

"Not only the owners," I said, "but most of the employees as well."

"Do you think they would like working with Germans?"

"Oh," I asked innocently, "are you German? ... I mean the name ..."

"Many people ask that," Pedro Olmo said, smiling. "You see, my father was Spanish and my mother German; I was born in Spain but grew up in Germany. Are the All-Ways people German Jews?" he asked, getting off the subject of himself.

"The owner, Saul Gurfein, although he has a German name, came originally from Russia, I think. So we have two cases in which the name doesn't tell the real story."

"What?"

"You both have German names and yours from Spain and his from Russia."

"Oh yes, a coincidence."

"What about prices, Roberto?" Kleinhuber said. "Do you think that they would be cheaper?"

I repeated what I had already told Kleinhuber about over-commissions for Olmo's benefit. I added that Lufthansa probably paid them even more over-commission than other airlines because they were interested in penetrating the Jewish market. "Jews have been reluctant to fly on Lufthansa, and they want to change that."

"Indeed? Why should they want to change it?" Olmo asked with an arched right eyebrow, I pretended not to get it.

"What do you mean?"

"Nada."

"Pedro has had some unpleasant experiences with Jewish businessmen," Kleinhuber tried to explain, "that's all." He turned to Olmo: "But there are all kinds of individuals, and if Herr Fox recommends these people, I think we should try them."

"You're the jefe," Olmo said, "but please remember that I must deal with them."

"And I think that will do you good, help you get over some of your prejudices."

Olmo glared at his boss, looked like he would continue to argue, thought better of it and said, "Perhaps you're right. Would you like to bet on the World Cup, Herr Fox?"

"Sure," I said, anxious to get away. "I'll take Brazil."

"And I Germany," Olmo said. "How about you, Wolfgang?"

"Argentina," Kleinhuber said. "And the winner will pay for lunch at the Club."

Olmo laughed, I grinned. "Gut, Wolfgang," he said. "I'll be glad to pay for betting on Germany's honor — and winning."

"This guy Pedro Olmo is as German as they come," I told Sara Romberg, "and has an unbelievable story about his father being Spanish and his mother German."

"It's possible," she interrupted.

"Anything is possible. That's not the point."

"Sorry I interrupted," she said. "What were you about to say?"

"You told me that Jessica Kutschmann is a teacher at the Steiner School."

"Yes."

"Pedro Olmo´s sister is also a teacher at that school," I said.

Her eyes widened, and she smiled for the first time since I'd met her.

"Wow! We're getting close, Roberto," she said. "If it is him, do you think Kleinhuber knows?"

"I don't know. But an innocent German doesn't change his name for nothing. Is there any chance of finding out the name on the passport the Vatican gave Kutschmann?"

She shook her head. "No, once they realized we were getting information from them, St. Peter closed the door to those archives and threw away the keys."

"... to the kingdom?" I added. "Sorry. How about Kutschmann's fingerprints?"

We were sitting on my balcony with the light of a full moon filtering through the high plane trees. Sara had come in a tight-fitting dress with a Chinese slit on the side. She looked much more appetizing than when I first met her fresh off a long-haul flight; more so even than the excellent pasta with mushroom sauce we had just finished. She took a sip of wine and thought for a moment. I was somewhat in love with her and she was, I could feel, ready to reciprocate. Whether it came to anything or not has nothing to do with this account, so I'll leave you to guess.

"If we don't already have them, we can get them," she said. "Do you have Olmo's prints?"

"I'm not a magician, but he might be an Argentine citizen."

"He almost certainly is," she confirmed. "These people want to get rid of the Vatican passports as quickly as possible."

"Right, good. So we can get his prints and match them with Kutschmann's."

"How?"

"It's not what you know around here." I looked at my watch. Midnight. Perfect. I brought my wireless phone to the table and dialed Comisario Alberto Contreras' number. His wife answered and I could hear a soccer game in the background on TV. After exchanging pleasantries, she called Alberto to the phone.

"Damn it, Zorro, can't a guy have some peace in his own home," he growled. Ever since he discovered that my name means zorro in Spanish, he loved to throw it at me when he was in a good mood.

"I know you're bored sitting there watching the idiot tube, my contrary friend, so I'm going to give you something interesting to think about."

"Go ahead and ruin my day."

Alberto is my contact in the Argentine Federal Police — a very good cop and an honest one. When he works with me, he gets credit for the arrest, if there is one, and cash when I'm paid for my efforts, which isn't always the case. "How'd you like to hunt a Nazi?"

"How'd you like to leave me out of politics for a change?"

"That's no answer."

"What have you got, Zorro?"

First, I told him what Kutschmann had done in Poland.

"A prick," was his only comment.

Then I gave him an abbreviated version of what I knew about Pedro Olmo.

"So what do you want from me?"

"Pedro Olmo is probably a naturalized citizen. Therefore, since the Federal Police — that's you — issues identity documents and passports, you should have his prints on file."

"Do you have Kutschmann's prints?"

"Not yet, but I will."

"I got news for you, Roberto," he said. "Those Nazi pricks got protection here; the bigger the prick the better the protection."

"I don't doubt it, Alberto, nor do I want to make it too easy for you."

"Gooooool!" screamed the TV. "Wait a mo," screamed Alberto. He was back in a few seconds. "Bueno, give me the prick's full name and whatever else you got," he said happily. Argentina must have scored. I nodded to Sara and smiled. She smiled back and placed her warm hand in mine.

The Wiesenthal Foundation didn't have Kutschmann's prints, so Wiesenthal had to use his influence to get them from the Nazi archives in Bonn. The bureaucracy there doesn't give anyone anything without a court order, which is time-consuming. Wiesenthal threatened the Justice Minister with complaining to the press that the government was protecting war criminals, and he got what he wanted schnell! Alberto Contreras used similar tactics to obtain Pedro Olmo's prints. To no one's surprise, they matched.

"The fucking Germans gotta ask us officially," Alberto told me, "first to arrest the guy we know as Pedro Olmo, then request extradition. They know how to do it through the German embassy here." They knew how, but they didn't do it. Andrea Gutiérrez made sure that the German embassy in Buenos Aires was informed. They then had to send all the evidence to Bonn that Walter Kutschmann, aka Pedro Olmos, wanted by the German Ministry of Justice for war crimes, had been positively identified. But the German embassy was without an ambassador at the moment, and the next highest diplomat, a guy named Werner Graf von Schulenburg, sat on the file for a week before asking the foreign office in Bonn for instructions. By the time Bonn answered Kutschmann was long gone, warned by someone in the German embassy or the Argentine police, or both. The pressure from his friends in the fascist Argentine military establishment was too great for Alberto Contrera's superiors.

When it was clear that Kutschmann was gone and the Argentine authorities had no interest in finding him, I sat with Alberto Contreras in a café in La Boca and listened to his lament. "That guy's got too many friends in high places,

Zorro. Don't ask me why, I don't know. I do what I'm told when this political crap is involved. They tell me stop, I stop. Sorry."

cIn case you're curious about Andrea Gutiérrez-Romberg and me, our relationship was intense but brief. I tried to convince her to stay with me in Argentina, but she was a woman with a mission: hunting Nazis. And although Argentina was a good hunting ground, her head office was in Vienna, and her heart was in Israel. She didn't have a third leg, so our love kindled, flared and, as absence doesn't really make the heart grow fonder, finally burned itself out.

*

This story is fiction but based on facts. Walter Kutschmann was arrested by the Argentine police in 1975 and later released because of Germany's delay in requesting his extradition. He subsequently disappeared but remained in Argentina. He died of natural causes in Buenos Aires many years later.

ANTHROPOSOPHICAL FANTASIES

The Ambassador's Son

Sometimes I woke up and didn't know where I was and what language I should say good morning to the maid in. I'd eat breakfast, usually alone, sometimes with my mother if she didn't get to bed late the night before, and head for school in a bulletproof, chauffeur-driven limousine with my two bodyguards. In case you didn't know, the United States is a big, unloved country that likes to throw its weight around so American companies can buy the world and the so-called Third World is full of assholes who think they can change everything by kidnapping the American ambassador's son.

I had this recurring dream. I'm spread-eagled naked on a cot in a dingy basement room. The terrorists decide that the only way to convince the United States to give Texas back to the Mexicans is to cut off my balls and send them to the White House with a note graphically stating what would be next. A hairless albino is approaching me with a hacksaw when I wake up screaming.

I thought what good is being an ambassador's son if all those assholes want to emasculate you to prove they mean business, and you have to be surrounded by bodyguards all the time. Also, I had a lot of discussions with my father about our supporting a military government whose hobby was "disappearing" anybody who didn't agree with them. He said it was all part of the war against communism — the usual bullshit. So I decided to quit being the ambassador's son, at least for a while.

That involved running away, which wasn't as easy as it sounds. A squad of Marines, a local security company and the police guarded the residence in Buenos Aires, and my two bodyguards always followed me like shadows. I had the advantage of surprise though, because they were there to protect me and weren't expecting me to want to escape.

I gave them the slip in the movies, where I went with the Liberian ambassador's daughter. "Look amigos," I said to my bodyguards, "I want to make out a little in the dark, so why don't you guys sit way in the back, so I don't get nervous from you breathing down my neck." The movie was with that Schwarzenegger meatloaf, just what they liked, and it served to distract them. I told the Liberian girl to tell my mother that I was fed up with being the ambassador's son and the stupid American school I had to attend, and I was taking a vacation for a while — just so they wouldn't think I'd been kidnapped and have my picture spread over every goddamn newspaper in the world.

I took a taxi to the city airport, which has domestic flights and some to neighboring counties; flights to and from more distant countries were at the international airport twenty miles from the city. I boarded a flight to Sao Paulo, Brazil. You'll probably ask why there, why not just lie low in Buenos Aires, which is as big as New York and just as easy to disappear in. Well, there's something I haven't mentioned yet. I'm black and my father was the only black American ambassador in the business. I don't want to get into racial shit here, but the fact is that Argentina has hardly any blacks to speak of. There used to be a lot, brought over from Africa as slaves, but they got killed off by cholera epidemics and fighting as conscripts in all the Indian wars they used to have, so I stuck out like a sore thumb. Also, I'm pretty well known because I dated some of the lily-white Argentine society girls and the newspapers thought that was news, which it was, because for an Argentine girl to date a black guy is like putting the purity of their fucking race in danger.

So, firstly, my best bet was to get out of Argentina so I wouldn't be recognized. Secondly, in Brazil every other dude is black, so I'd not only not be recognized there but would blend in colorwise as well. Thirdly, I knew a place to go where they'd never think of looking for me: a *favela*, which is Brazilian for a shantytown. And fourthly, I speak fluent Brazilian Portuguese, better even than Spanish, because that's where my dad was stationed last and I spent some very formative years there.

When my father was ambassador to Brazil, we visited a favela once in Sao Paulo because the U.S. government donated some computers to a school there. He wanted to show me how generous we were and how we were helping the poor and all that crap, when actually all were doing was making it worse. I mean they're starving so we give them computers. During that visit we saw some young people there: Germans, a Swiss and even a couple of Americans who worked temporarily as volunteers. I intended to offer myself as a volunteer there until I got tired of it.

Dona Ute (pronounced **oo**-teh), the woman who ran the school, lived in a house that wasn't much better than the ones in the favela. It was perched on a hill overlooking the *avenida*, which meant you couldn't hear yourself think because of the racket the buses and cars made. There was no bell, so I clapped my hands, which is what you do in Brazil when there's no bell.

I remembered her, though I knew she wouldn't remember me. She barely looked at me back then, because everyone was so excited about the American ambassador, thinking it was a big deal, which it wasn't. My father never said a word to the favela people, he didn't even look at them. He talked to Dona Ute a little, but mostly he hung onto the Mayor of Sao Paulo, who's now in jail on a money laundering charge, and the press of course. Dona Ute wasn't old or anything, but she looked kind of bedraggled, like something the cat dragged in. But I admired her a million times more than those ambassadors' wives who always look like they just stepped out of a beauty parlor.

I was tempted to say I was Brazilian, but decided it wasn't a good idea because there are always little things that can give you away if you're not a real native, like who won the soccer championship in 1940, because soccer is a subject Brazilians are absolutely nuts about. I knew who Pelé and Maradona were and that's about it. I really like baseball, but what good is that in Brazil where they wouldn't recognize a fast ball if it hit them in the face. So, I decided to play it safe and say I was an American who lived in Brazil a number of years until my father, a missionary, got transferred back to the States and now I'm a student doing my thesis about the Brazilian favelas. Pretty thin, when I think about it now, but they swallowed it.

"You know that we can't pay you," Dona Ute said, "except carfare if you have to go someplace for us."

"That's all right, I don't need money."

"Your Portuguese is very good. Do you know other

languages?"

"English of course."

"Of course."

"Then there's Spanish, German, French, Hindustani. That's about it."

"Enough," she laughed. "How did you learn all those languages?"

"Oh, my dad was stationed all over the place and I just picked them up. Kids can do that, so I'm not bragging"

"Yes, I know. I also led a nomadic life as a child," Dona Ute said. "My father was a scientist, and we lived in many different countries. I think that being rootless as a child does something to you. In a sense it's positive; in another sense it deprives you of something."

"In your case it was positive," I said.

She sighed. "Please don't think I'm some kind of Mother Teresa. It isn't true, and I wouldn't like it."

"OK, I won't." But I did.

"We'd like to send our appeals to more places in the people's own languages," Dona Ute said. "Maybe you could work in the office and do that."

"Sure," I said, really pleased, because I wasn't looking forward to wiping kids' asses all day.

"One or two days a week. There are other things to do outside the office."

"Oh sure, I wouldn't want to be cut off from the real work."

"That's the spirit," she said, and I knew I had made a good

impression.

"Our work is inspired by Anthroposophy," dona Ute said. "Do you know what that is?"

I'd never heard of Anthroposophy, but I figured I'd lied enough for one day, so I told her the truth: "No."

"It's a spiritual, education and social movement begun more than a hundred years ago in Germany." Dona Ute smiled. "But I won't go into that now; if it interests you, we can talk about it later. Oh, by the way, what's your name?"

Believe it or not I wasn't prepared for that question; I only hesitated for a second though.

"Jackie."

"Jackie what?"

"Jackie Robinson."

It was inspiration. I realized too late that it could draw the attention of Americans looking for me, but once I said it I was glad because I really loved that guy. And like I said, Brazilians aren't interested in baseball, so they wouldn't recognize the name of the first black player in major league history.

A Brazilian guy name of Zeca, a couple of years older than me and a political science student, worked in the "office" — just a shack tacked into the school — doing most of the administrative work. He looked like a mixture of all the races in the world. I helped him with letters in other languages. He asked me a lot about the States, especially the condition of blacks. My family is very integrated into white society. I mean we hardly even *know* any blacks, except for my relatives. What I told him was more than he knew though, and he seemed satisfied. He asked me what I thought about the social situation in Brazil, and I told him it was terrible, that's why I was there, to help with what little I could, which was bullshit of course, but he believed me.

One day when we were alone in the office he said, without looking up from what he was doing, "Hey, Jackie, do you think what we're doing will change anything?"

It was a good question, one I hadn't considered before. "We're helping the kids in this favela," I said.

"Wake up, Jackie. Brazil has about 130 million people and two-thirds of them live like animals. So what good is helping a few people in one privileged favela?"

"Why do you work here then?"

"Because I used to think like you, that it's better than nothing and now I'm here and I'm not so sure anymore."

I didn't say anything, not that I had anything to say anyway.

"I like you, Jackie. You're a gringo, you can't help that, but at least you're black and you've got a social conscience, or you wouldn't be here." He turned back to his work, but I suspected he'd have more to say about all that soon, and I was right.

I got to know a lot of people in the favela, but the most important person for me was Mireya, a black girl of only fifteen. The guys said she was stuck-up. I thought that too until I saw her with the kids in the kindergarten where she worked as an assistant. I fell in love with her, which was wonderful, but it complicated things considerably. In order to get to work in the kindergarten I told Dona Ute that I was crazy about little kids, which wasn't exactly true. I have this little brother that I'm not too crazy about because, frankly, he's a spoiled brat. I guess that's not his fault though, considering the rest of my family. My real reason was to be near Mireya. It was kind of rough at first because favela kids aren't spoiled, they're rotten. If one of them gets his hands on a toy you can't get it away from him without threats. And what manners! They eat like it was the first time they ever saw food. But I guess if you were always hungry, you'd act the same way.

I started to walk Mireya home, with the excuse that she could tell me on the way about how I could improve my work in kindergarten. She lived with her mother and uncle and four smaller brothers and sisters in a miserable hut in the favela, but at least it was clean, which is more than you could say for most of the others. You think that favelas are dangerous, right? Well, they are. Drug dealers, thieves, murderers, you name it. Not the majority though. Believe it or not, the majority of people who live there are honest and religious. Their religion is weird though, being a mixture of *Macumba*, which is a kind of good voodoo, and Catholic. But there are a lot of low-lifes around, so it *is* dangerous. But not for Dona Ute's people. We could come and go as we pleased, and nobody bothered us. That's because they considered Dona Ute to be some kind of saint. And it's not smart to mess with saints. The crooks even gave her a computer (stolen of course), which she didn't accept because she thought she could be encouraging crime by taking it. When Zeca found out he told them to put it in the office, and he'd handle Dona Ute. His way of handling her was not to mention it. She saw it there, but she didn't say anything either. After all, a donation is a donation. Zeca said we accepted donations from companies who exploit the poor and even from the United States, who are imperialists, etc., so why not from a poor favela thief who only stole from the rich.

One night I took Mireya to see a movie. We went to a pizza parlor afterwards and I asked her how much school she had, and she said primary school.

"Don't you want to go to high school?"

"Yes, of course, but I have to take care of my brothers and sisters because my mother works all day."

"What does she do?"

"She's a maid for a rich family."

Rich is relative, because for the favela dwellers everyone who lives outside the favela is rich. But rich or not, they all have maids, because in Brazil you can always find someone poorer than you who's willing to work for next to nothing.

"That's too bad," I said, "because if you don't go to high school you'll probably end up being a maid, too."

"What's wrong with being a maid?"

"Nothing. If you think they're so great you can be one."

She cried then, which made me feel sorry for what I said, especially when she explained that she didn't have money for carfare or books.

"Look, Mireya," I said, "maybe something can be worked out for you to go at night. Did you ever talk to Dona Ute about it?"

"She says I should go to school too."

"Don't they give you any money for working in the kindergarten?"

"Yes, but I give it to my mother. Besides, the night school is two hours away by bus. I'd have to spend four hours just traveling."

"That's because it makes so many detours and stops at every puddle. If you went in the minivan ..."

"The minivan? But I can't drive, I'm too young."

"I'm not." I smiled and put my hand on hers, the one that wasn't holding a piece of pizza.

"You'd take me to school every night?"

"Sure, why not?" I didn't have a Brazilian driver's license, only my Argentine one, but that's valid in Brazil if you're a tourist. It's under my real name, but I didn't expect to get stopped because I drive real careful compared to Brazilians who drive like maniacs. Besides, the only reason the cops stop anybody is to shake them down, so they wouldn't be interested in a black kid driving a favela-school minivan.

Mireya said OK, but one night a week she couldn't go to school because she had to go to a meeting. I thought at first that it was a meeting about Anthroposophy, the spiritual movement Dona Ute told me about. Mireya asked if I'd like to go to the meetings too. Well, whatever Anthroposophy is, it didn't sound very exciting, and I had avoided going to lectures some friends of Ute's gave, but now that I knew that Mireya went to meetings, my attitude changed. I asked her if they were about Anthroposophy and she said, "Sort of" — which tuned out to be an under or an overstatement, depending on how you look at it.

Dona Ute not only agreed to lend us the minivan but also said the school would pay for Mireya's books because it was important that future teachers have a good education. So, Mireya enrolled in night school and I took her there every weeknight except Thursdays, when we went to the meetings.

During the three hours I had to wait for her on school days I went to a cafe and read books or wrote this sort of diary. I threw a lot away, the boring stuff. Maybe I shouldn't have, but I don't like to read boring stuff, even if it's written by me. But there is one thing I'd like to mention, even though it doesn't have much to do with what happened later, I mean the kidnapping and all.

One day just before Easter, Mireya asked me if I was going to the *Santa Ceia*.

"What's that?"

"Come to the *Escolinha*" — that's what they call Dona Ute's school — "at seven o'clock. You'll see."

The *Escolinha* was a big barrack-like prefab that they'd fixed up nice by painting it and hanging pictures and with plants and so forth. I didn't hear any noise as I approached at about seven-fifteen, so I thought there was nobody there yet. But when I pushed open the side door I walked into a full house. Cido, a young *favelado* who worked in the carpentry shop, was standing dressed like a priest behind a table covered with a blue cloth. I thought it must be a play, which they were fond of doing, so I sat down at a table near the door and watched. At the same table, or altar I should say, but seated, was Dona Ute and at either side altar boys stood straight like bookends.

Cido was finishing reading something. He handed the book to the boy on his left, who read falteringly. It was the Bible, and he was reading about Jesus being condemned to die. Then he passed the book to the boy on his right, who read about Jesus' resurrection. When he finished Dona Ute held up a large photograph of a boy. She said that the boy had died in an accident and his father, a lawyer, didn't know what to do with the insurance money he received because he didn't need it. Then he heard about Dona Ute's work, so he sent the money to her and that's how they were able to buy the land and put up the prefab that served as a school. She asked us to pray for the boy and his father. Cido closed his eyes and said a prayer, and everyone closed their eyes and bowed their heads, so I did too. I wasn't really praying, but I didn't want to be the only one staring into space. Then what really surprised me was that Cido took some bread from a basket and said, "This is my body", then he lifted up a glass of what looked like wine and blessed it and said, "This is my blood." Then some kids with baskets went around putting a piece of bread in front of each person sitting at the tables. We already had empty glasses, most of them chipped, in front of us, and more kids came and filled them with wine. At first I thought it was funny that they were giving those little kids wine, but when I tasted it, I realized it was water with about one drop of wine in it. Well, we all ate the bread and drank the wine, but it was like a party, people talking and laughing and everything.

I know what a mass is, because they tried to bring me up Catholic, but what I witnessed in the favela was what it might have been like way back when people still remembered Jesus and it hadn't yet been turned into a torture for little kids where you have to confess how many times you jerked off before you can eat a little piece of dry bread and you don't get any wine at all.

I asked Dona Ute about it afterwards. She told me how there was a shortage of priests in Brazil so in many towns the oldest son in a respected family plays the part. They don't consider it a mass really, she explained. I said no, it's better. She just laughed and changed the subject.

Mireya and I got a lot closer, but even when we were alone in my room, I never had sex with her, although I guess I could have. We kissed and I fondled her breasts and kissed them. They were like little brown apples and tasted a million times better. I told her I loved her, and she smiled and touched my cheek and said she loved me too. Dona Ute said she hoped my relationship with Mireya was a responsible one, that she was only a child and all that. I said sure, not to worry, and it was true, I wasn't lying about that. I mean what we were doing was kid stuff compared to what goes on.

On Thursday night we went to the meeting. Zeca resided and made a big deal about me being there, saying I was a black gringo with a social conscience, and I would be a welcome and invaluable addition to the group. Zeca could talk, no doubt about it. They went on about why the poor were poor and what Rudolf Steiner said about it and what a great hero Che Guevara was and all that crap. I sat there not saying anything until Zeca asked me what I thought. I should have kept my trap shut, but I have this problem that whenever anyone asks me what I think I tell them.

"What's it have to do with Anthroposophy?" I asked him.

"Everything," Zeca answered. "Anthroposophy isn't only meditation and angels and Jesus and stuff, it's also about education and the threefold social organism."

"what's that?"

"It's how society should function, but doesn't: equality in the political state sphere, fraternity in the economic sphere and freedom in the spiritual-cultural sphere. The big problem is that they're all bunched up and the economy — big business — runs everything." He went on for another half hour explaining how he understood the concept. "See what I mean?" he concluded.

"It's interesting," I said, "but so what? I mean what can we do about it?"

"We have a plan," Zeca said, and exhaled a perfect smoke-ring. "We're going to kidnap the American ambassador's daughter."

I didn't physically fall off my chair, but mentally I did.

"It's a bold move," Zeca went on, "but we must do something bold to show that we exist and that we mean business."

"But why her?" I knew her pretty well. She was a couple of years older than me, a student at some Ivy League University. She thought she was hot shit because she was older and pretty and white and could beat me at chess, but that's only because she had been stationed in Russia where they learn to play in school. I would have liked to do something else with her besides play chess, but she never paid much attention to me, maybe because she wasn't too keen on crossing the color line.

"A friend of mine who's an exchange student at the university she goes to in the United States knows her," Zeca explained. "He says she has a social conscience."

I doubted that very much.

"Look," Zeca went on, excited, "we bring her to a safe house and explain the situation in Brazil to her. We don't hurt her or ask for money or anything like that. It's a purely political act. Her disappearance will make world headlines. Then we release her, and she tells the world what we want."

"And what's that?"

"Justice, a new order, the threefold social organism."

"How are you going to kidnap her if she's in the States?"

"She comes to Brazil during vacations."

"Does she speak Portuguese?" I didn't think she did.

"We're not sure. That's why we need you, Jackie. What do you say?"

"I think it's crazy," which was my honest opinion. "Count me out." Then came the touch that changed my life. Mireya put her hand on my knee, which was bare because we all wore shorts and said, "Please, Jackie, at least think about it."

But the more I thought about it the crazier it seemed. "Let's suppose you succeed in grabbing her. What do you do with her? The Brazilian police and armed forces will be looking for her, not to mention the CIA, FBI and a million people looking for the reward they'll offer."

"We have a place where they won't find her."

"Where?"

"He's not one of us," a big black guy protested, "not a Brazilian who feels with our suffering people."

"Che wasn't a Cuban," a cross-eyed white girl said.

"No, and who knows how long it took to convince him," Zeca agreed. "But once he decided to help, he became the heart of Latin American revolution, transcending Fidel, just *because* he wasn't Cuban." He looked at me as though he thought he was Fidel Castro about to recruit Che Guevara to the cause. "This may be the beginning of the liberation of your own people, Jackie."

"Where are you going to hide her?" I asked, still hoping

to convince them that the idea was crazy.

"In a *fazenda* an hour's drive from Sao Paulo."

"So what's so secure about that?" A fazenda is a Brazilian farm.

Zeca looked at a big hairy white guy sitting next to him, who nodded. "It belongs to the Commanding General of the Sao Paulo Military Area."

"Zeca, are you trying to tell me that a *general* is in with you on this?"

"No, and he hasn't been to his fazenda in three years. His son, Socrates," — he indicated the white guy with his head — "lives there."

I didn't know what to say. If they could really hide her in a general's house ...

"Would she see our faces?" I asked.

"Of course not. We'll be masked."

I should have stood up then, said OK, count me in comrades, and gone straight to the airport to take the first plane to Miami. But I didn't. Instead, I asked how they planned to get the ambassador's daughter to the fazenda.

"Are you with us, or not?" Zeca asked. They were all staring at me expectantly, especially Mireya. Zeca had told me where they planned to keep the girl, a show of confidence on their part. My main concern was what Mireya would think of me if I said no; second was whether they'd let me walk out of there knowing what I now knew.

I gave the thumbs-up sign, which means the same in Brazil as it does everywhere else, except that in Brazil everybody's always using it. Zeca smiled and gave it back to me and so did the rest and we all sat there like idiots with our thumbs up.

"She lives in Brasilia when she's here of course," Zeca explained, "but comes to Sao Paulo often and stays with a Brazilian boyfriend. We watch the boyfriend and when they go out at night we wait for the right opportunity and when it comes, well, it shouldn't be too difficult."

"What about bodyguards?"

"There's only one and she usually gives him the slip. He doesn't say anything, probably because it would cost him his job if he did, or maybe he doesn't mind having some time off."

We had the minivan because it was a school night, and Mireya rode huddled close to me on the way home. I asked her up to my room, even though it was late, and we went to bed. But I didn't do anything if that's what you're thinking. What the hell, she was only fifteen and I had promised Dona Ute.

A month passed and nobody said anything about the kidnapping. Mireya even went to school on meeting night. I hoped they'd decided the idea was too crazy and had given it up; but that was wishful thinking.

"We got the girl," Zeca told me one day when we were alone in the office.

"What girl?" I asked, hoping it wasn't true.

"The ambassador's daughter, stupid." And he laughed like the maniac he was.

"How?"

"In the movies. The theater was almost empty last night.

When the movie ended the boyfriend left her in front of the theater while he went to get his car that was parked on the next street. All we had to do was push her into the minivan before he got back and drive away. I don't think anyone even noticed it."

"You used the *minivan*?"

"We covered up the name," Zeca smiled. "Don't worry."

"So she's at the fazenda now?"

"That's right. And she doesn't speak Portuguese."

"How do you know?"

"I asked her."

"Maybe she was lying."

"Why should she lie about that?"

I didn't know.

"Tonight, after you take Mireya to school you go right to the fazenda." He took a piece of paper from his pocket and handed it to me. "Here's a map. It's easy to get there. It'll take you about a half-hour."

"What am I supposed to do?"

"She's pretty scared. I thought you could tell her you're a gringo too and explain why you're fighting with us."

"I don't think that's a good idea."

"Why not?"

"It'd be better if I'm Brazilian, so they can't trace me later."

Zeca thought a while, then said, "Maybe you're right," but he didn't sound convinced.

I felt sick, to tell the truth. I was thinking of how I could disguise myself. Zeca said there was a ski mask in the minivan that I should put on when I got to the fazenda. I could try to fake an accent. I even thought of disguising the fact that I'm black, but that was impossible. I mean I couldn't very well wear a jump suit and gloves when everyone else is walking around in shorts. She might think I was the invisible man and if I took off my clothes there wouldn't be anything there.

I drove to the fazenda that night after dropping Mireya off at school. It was one of those really huge properties full of cows and stuff and a house that Trump wouldn't mind living in, the kind that generals somehow get to own despite their lousy salaries. I rang the bell and Socrates, the general's son, opened the door and gave me the thumbs-up sign.

"She's upstairs in the master bedroom," he said, and led the way up a curving staircase. I put the mask on, took a deep breath and went in.

She was propped up on the bed with her knees up reading a book by Stephen King. I could see a piece of her black panties that contrasted with the inside of her white thighs. She glanced over the book and said, "Don't you guys ever knock?" She straightened out her legs, so the best part of the view was gone, but it was pretty good anyway. She was wearing a miniskirt and a tight sleeveless polo shirt without a bra so her nipples popped out like cherry pits. I went over to the bed and stood beside it. The room was big and bare. They'd removed everything that would have allowed her to identify the room.

"What do you want?" she asked nervously, despite the show of bravado.

"Don't worry," I said with a phony Brazilian accent.

"Nobody's going to harm you."

"Fine, but I asked you what you want."

"I want to talk to you about ... er ... certain things."

She looked at me kind of funny, like she noticed something about me.

"You're probably wondering why you're here."

"I'm here because you bastards kidnapped me."

"We didn't kidnap you, we just want to talk to you."

"What's the difference? ... Hey, are you a Brazilian, or what?"

"Yes, I am."

"How come you speak such good English then?"

"I lived in the States a while. Besides, lots of Brazilians speak good English."

"Not *black* Brazilians."

Bitch!

"How come that other creep said a gringo would come to see me then?"

"Well ... er ... they call me gringo because I lived in the States."

"Hmm. Hey, do you play chess?" she asked, trying to look through my mask.

"No. Black Brazilians don't play chess."

She smiled. "Ever been to Buenos Aires?"

So, she recognized me despite the mask and the phony accent, but could she be sure? I considered trying to bluff my way through but decided against it, because what if she told Zeca who I was, or who she thought I was. He'd laugh, but then he'd damn sure find out.

"OK Alice, just listen a minute. We're in this together and we gotta play it smart or we'll never get out alive." That impressed her all right; she stared at me with her mouth open. "These people think I'm an American preacher's son who lived in Brazil and learned the language and now I'm working in a favela because of my social conscience. They got this idea to kidnap you, and they asked me to join them and I went along to make sure nothing happens to you."

"But what are you doing here?"

"I ran away from the embassy in Buenos Aires."

"What'd you run away for?" She was looking at me funny as though she didn't believe me up to then and was prepared not to believe what I would say to her last question.

"I just got fed up with all the diplomatic horseshit. You know what I mean."

"I do? Hey, why don't you take off that stupid mask? I know who you are anyway, Booker Tee."

I don't believe I mentioned yet that my real name is Booker T. Washington Smith. A psychologist would probably tell you that I didn't mention it till now because I don't like it, and he'd be right. I have absolutely nothing against Booker T. Washington, in fact I admire him. But that doesn't mean they had to name me after him. It's a pretentious name, another reason why I prefer Jackie Robinson.

"One of those guys could walk in any minute," I whispered. "And don't call me Booker Tee, for God's sake."

"What should I call you, Zorro?"

"Yeah, that's fine." I didn't mind that name at all.

"I'll turn off the light," Alice said. "Then nobody'll know if you're wearing the mask or not."

She switched off the night-table lamp before I could object. A slip of light rolled under the door from the hall outside and lamplight from the garden diffused itself through the closed shutters, but it was dark enough not to know whether I was wearing the ski-mask or not, so I took it off. I could see Alice's blonde hair and white skin though. She slid her ass over until she was sitting in front of me with her skirt pushed up to her hips from sliding like that. She took my hand and pulled me down beside her.

"Do they want money?"

"No, just publicity, then they'll let you go."

"I know you'll watch out for me, Book ... Zorro." She giggled and let her head sink onto my shoulder, and she put her hand on my naked thigh, just below the bottom of my shorts.

I was in love with Mireya, like I said, but as you probably know, adolescents are about the horniest toads around. I wasn't screwing Mireya because she was a minor, so when Alice, who was of age, started to fool around like that I got a hard-on that couldn't possibly stay inside my shorts, so I opened them, and it jumped out like a rocket on its way to Mars. And when Alice went down on it I came in less time than it takes to say Booker T. Washington Smith. She went into the bathroom, to spit it out I guess, and when she came back, she was naked and straddled me before my rocket collapsed. Since I had just come, I was able to hold out indefinitely and we rolled around the bed in an orgy with Alice moaning "Again, Zorro, again, please!" and me trying to shut her up and liking it at the same time. It was obvious that she had a lot of experience with sex. It goes to show what an Ivy League education can do for you.

When I finally left the room and ran downstairs, Socrates asked me how it went, and I said it went fine. "Does she really have a social conscience?" he asked.

I had forgotten all about that. "I think she may, but we've got to play it cool, not rush her." Socrates gave me the old thumb-up and I jumped into the minivan and somehow made it back to Mireya's school. She said she'd been worried about me, which made me feel like the turd I was.

"How did it go?" Zeca asked me in the office the next day.

"Pretty good, I think. I want her to trust me first of all and get to the serious stuff later."

"How much later?"

"Soon, maybe tonight if I think she's ready."

"As soon as possible, Jackie." He looked around, although we were the only ones in the room and the door squeaked like ten cats when someone opened it.

I had been thinking a lot about how to handle Alice. If I wanted her to come over to our side — I know, I'm saying "our" side now, because that's the way it turned out — the only way to do it was to keep on screwing her. I figured it was the only thing she gave a shit about, because she thought it was Love. But love is what I felt for Mireya, who I couldn't screw because she was too young and even if she weren't I'd have to go on screwing Alice in order to get her on our side. It's what my father would call a dilemma — one of his favorite words.

The next night I started to talk to Alice about the condition of the poor in Brazil. "Do you realize that seventy per cent of the population is poor and half of them live in abject poverty?" (I modified Zeca's statistics a little because I figured they were exaggerated, though I didn't really know.) "The favelas are hotbeds of crime, perversion, drugs, violence. The children don't have a chance. They live on beans and rice and are undernourished, hardly go to school, are often sexually abused and the great majority of them become street children, first begging, then stealing, they become drug addicts and pushers, are often tortured and killed by the police. And do you know who's responsible?" Alice's eyes were saying: "What do I care, do it again, Zorro." So I did. She said she loved my brown skin, meaning she loved my black pecker.

"And you know who's responsible?" I repeated after an indecent interval.

"The government?"

"Not only. You and me and our fucking ambassador fathers who only protect American business interests. And the fucking capitalists, all of them, the American ones, the Brazilians, Germans, all of them." Boy, I was sounding like Zeca.

Suddenly, I mean *suddenly*, the door crashed open and there were about twenty Military Police in the room shouting and pointing their guns at us. Alice and I were still naked in bed. I sat up and she pulled the sheet over her head. They dragged me out of the bed and one of them punched me, breaking my nose. An officer screamed into his cellular phone that they'd found the American ambassador's daughter and her kidnapper.

"No, It's a mistake, I'm the —" I tried to talk spitting blood, but the soldier who punched me told me to shut up or he'd break my ass as well. So I shut up.

They took me to one of their interrogation rooms, still naked, and a fat guy said I should tell them who my accomplices were, or he'd stick the red-hot poker he was holding up my ass. It was my nightmare come true.

"I'm the American ambassador to Argentina's son," I said in Portuguese with a phony American accent, trying to sound calm, although I was trembling like a guy who was about to have a red-hot poker shoved up his ass.

The four goons in the room dropped their four imbecile jaws. Then the fat one began to laugh, and his belly shook as he approached me with the poker reflected in his bloodshot eyes.

"Wait a minute!" The officer, who I hadn't noticed because he was behind me, came to the front and stared at me. He probably remembered that the previous ambassador to Brazil had been black. I don't think he believed me, but he wasn't taking any chances.

"Don't touch him," he said to the fat one, "at least not until I come back."

Fatso didn't like being deprived of his fun and he made a face, so the officer grabbed him by his shirt front and told him if he touched me, he'd be boiled in his own fat. The officer was a little skinny guy, but it shows what authority can do.

It wasn't more than an hour, I guess, but it seemed a lot longer, when the officer returned with two Americans wearing pinstriped ties and short-sleeved shirts. One was a vice consul, and the other didn't say who he was — probably CIA. They questioned me, and I gave all the right answers — about who I was, not about the kidnapping. When they started on that I asked them what Alice told them, and they said she was in shock. I told them to get me some clothes and get me out of that place. They borrowed a pair of shorts somehow and when we left, I looked at Fatso and the one who broke my nose and said, in my best low Portuguese, "I'll remember you two pricks." Then we drove to the German hospital — the best in town — where they fixed my nose, although I guess it'll always be crooked.

Luckily, Alice was in the same hospital. She didn't know what to say about the kidnapping and me, so she had just kept her trap shut and they thought she was in shock. At first, they didn't want to let me see her, but I said maybe I could help her so they let me. There was a doctor and a woman from the embassy present, not to mention Alice's mother, who was sitting in the corner looking like she just came out of a beauty parlor.

"Alice, darling, I think we have to tell the truth," I said, taking her hand. Things were pretty complicated for her. The Brazilian boyfriend turned out to be a famous soccer player, married to a movie star, a detail that Zeca had neglected to mention. When Alice disappeared in front of the theater the boyfriend decided to disappear too. Alice told me all that later.

"I mean that friend of mine, you know, Socrates? loaned us the house in the fazenda so we could be together for the weekend."

"Oh, Zorro, I'm so glad you're here," she cried and grabbed me around the neck and kissed me.

"Zorro!" her mother cried. "Who's Zorro?"

I was released the next morning when my father came, and he shipped me off to a military school in Virginia where I did my senior high school year. It was a crock of shit, but I was an ambassador's son, so no one bothered me much. I promised my father I'd stay if he agreed to let me go to the University of Sao Paulo — finance me, that is, because I wouldn't be a minor by then. Finally, he said OK, probably because USP is a lot cheaper than Georgetown or the Ivy League.

Once back in Brazil I made sure that Mireya finished high school and went to college. I also made sure that she stayed clear of kidnappings and that kind of stuff. There are other ways to change things, like what Dona Ute is doing. I made a list in my diary of all the things I like about Brazil. Most of them are predictable, like Mireya and Dona Ute and thumbs-up and the racial mixture and the mass that's better than a real one, and all the people walking around in shorts and smiling despite being so poor. I know it sounds crazy, but up near the top of the list, right below Mireya and Dona Ute, is one of the things I like most about Brazil: that they call me Jackie Robinson here.

After school I stayed in Brazil. My grandfather had become rich founding a recording company in Harlem that specialized in jazz and soul, and he left me a million dollars in his will. I had told him about the favela and how they called me Jackie Robinson and he wanted me to be able to stay here and help. So I did. Dona Ute began a school with a clinic in a favela in Rio and asked me to run it, together with Mireya.

Although Brazilians aren't interested in baseball, you can watch games on pay TV. So that's what Mireya and I were doing on Jackie Robinson Day. I tried to explain the game to her, but it wasn't easy. She knows my real name now of course but still calls me Jackie.

ANTHROPOSOPHICAL FANTASIES

by Roberto Fox

The Occult Inquisitor

A modern parable

by Shirley Locke-Holmes — as told to Frank Thomas Smith

No one knows where the woman came from, she just appears one day in the small Swiss town. It's springtime and she is dressed in a light, attractive frock reaching to just below her knees. As she passes the vegetarian restaurant on the corner the people eating lunch in the garden stare at her, then go out to greet her, hesitantly at first, then in a rush: students carrying notebooks, old people wearing black berets, even the waitresses and the cook with a frying pan in his hand. She smiles warmly at them, then turns left up the hill towards the temple. They follow her. The few people who live in the house halfway between the restaurant and the temple join the throng, as do those who are in its small art gallery. The word spreads quickly and people run from all the houses on and near the hill to follow her. The strange thing is that they all, without being told or having seen her before, recognize her.

She pauses in front of the temple for a moment, shakes her head sadly, and continues up into the woods beyond it. When she reaches a clearing sufficiently large to accommodate the crowd she stops, takes off her knapsack and places it on the ground, shakes out her long black hair and smiles at the people. She motions for them to sit and they do so, forming a circle around her. She begins to speak in a beautifully modulated voice. They listen hungrily, for this is real spiritual knowledge.

She returns to the same place the next day and the crowd of listeners has grown enormously. On the third day the Chairman of the Society, who has been informed of her presence, comes to the scene accompanied by some other functionaries of the Society and a policeman. They push their way through to the front using elbows, knees and authority. After listening to her for a while the Chairman knits his gray, beetling brows and his eyes flash. Suddenly he shouts for her to be silent. The listeners do not protest, for they are used to bowing to authority. The Chairman tells the policeman to seize her, charged with trespassing, but to bring her to his office in the temple where he will look into the matter.

He makes her wait for an hour in his antechamber before summoning her to enter his organically-shaped, purple-trimmed office with its elongated floor-to-ceiling windows. He sits at his large, liver-shaped desk and motions for her to sit across from him.

"Who are you?" he asks angrily, but she doesn't reply. She looks out the window at the gray granite of the Jura hills.

"That's right, be silent. I don't want to know who you are. But if you are Him, I must inform you that your arrival here at this particular point in time is inappropriate, unwanted, even dangerous. You see, the work of the Society is centered in the Board of Directors [Vorstand] here in the temple. It's the centralized organization which you yourself called into existence during the Foundation Meeting way back in 1923." She raises her eyebrows slightly, a movement he does not fail to notice.

"Oh, I suppose you would say that you didn't intend it that way, that you had quite a different organization in mind". He laughs, his mouth twisting into a cynical smile.

"Did you seriously think that something so confusing, chaotic and anarchical could possibly work? My dear man — I mean woman — How could you be so naive? We knew it wouldn't work, and we took care to keep the members ignorant of your foolishness. As you probably know, all the members of the Society were incorporated into the General Society in 1925, and they weren't even aware of it. Are these the sheep you expected to act in freedom? Don't make me laugh! Just think: you formulated the statutes of the Society, which you called the most modern society in the world, then you said they weren't statutes at all, but a reality. Who can make heads or tails of such a mess? We solved the problem though — after you died of course, so you couldn't confuse the matter further — by calling those original statutes 'principles' and absorbing everything and everyone into the General Society, a legally constituted unprofitable — er, I mean not-for-profit corporation with power vested in the Board and proper statutes that anyone can understand."

The woman continues gazing out the window. The Chairman smiles crookedly and goes on.

"In case you're wondering why I say 'we' when I wasn't even born then, I ask you to remember that apostolic succession — well, succession at least — is an esoteric tradition that we have maintained since you passed over the threshold, despite the fact that you failed to name your successor."

She turns her head toward him and seems about to say something but remains silent.

"You were probably upset about all the expulsions back in the thirties," the Chairman goes on. "After all, they were your friends and collaborators. It was unfortunate but necessary, although I might have handled it differently. Those friends of yours who were expelled refused to recognize the Chairman's authority. And even you must realize how dangerous that was. Independent societies springing up all over the place, no clarity, no central authority. Oh, it was done smoothly enough. My predecessors called it 'self-expulsion', a stroke of genius. Just between you and me, I think the Soviets got the idea from us. All the General Assembly had to do was sanction their requests — admittedly unspoken — for self-expulsion. Now please tell me how that could have been done under your wishy-washy statutes, which don't even contain a provision for expulsion? You should thank us for picking up the pieces and gluing them back together. If we hadn't, nothing would be left of your work. Don't you realize that?" He becomes red in the face. "Don't you? Answer me!" he shouts and slams his fist on the desk, causing the portrait of the temple's founder hanging on the wall to fall to the floor behind him. She doesn't answer him. Gradually he calms down, rises, picks up the portrait and places it back on the wall. The solid wood organically carved frame had saved it from breaking. "It's not the first time this has happened. This thing is indestructible," the Chairman mumbles.

Once seated again he says, "Then there was the unpleasant incident with your wife. We couldn't convince the Swiss judges that your literary estate belongs to us, to the Society, and not to an individual, last will or no last will. We lost that round — two rounds actually — and now they've published almost everything you ever wrote or said, most of it as confusing as ever. We would have been more selective, retaining the more powerful stuff for ourselves. But a lot has changed: we even sell your books at the temple bookshop now. Imagine!

"Speaking of powerful stuff — the Esoteric lectures. For a long time, we managed to protect them, just as you wished. Now even they have been published by your so-called literary estate. But this time it's been done with our blessing. And why not? Why fight a losing battle? They would have published them anyway. It's a feather plucked from our cap all right, but we still control the School, including membership and expulsion. It's much easier to expel someone from the School than from the Society, as you know. No fuss. And that gives us a lot of leverage. Membership in the School has increased enormously, by the way, thanks to us. That doesn't mean they're all initiates — ha, ha. We launched very successful membership drives and soon almost all Society members will also be members of the School. If you want to be in the 'in-group', it's the thing to do, believe me."

She frowns.

"Ah, a reaction at last. I suppose you're worried about the esoteric development of all those people. Forget it. All that stuff you said and wrote about initiation doesn't work. I know, I tried it.

"We have our critics of course. Some time ago an old guy — probably one of your friends — called the School Readers the 'curia'. Thought he was being smart; I'd call him fresh.

"There has even been criticism of the fact that I travel first-class on airplanes and stay at five-star hotels. It just shows how niggardly they are, or maybe it's only jealousy.

People don't realize that we must arrive refreshed after a long journey, sleep in a comfortable bed and have all the necessary conveniences at our fingertips: telephone, TV, FAX, e-mail, swimming pool, masseur, hairdresser — in order to faithfully carry your message to the antipodes. Whoever heard of an executive of an organization of over 50,000 traveling economy class and living in hovels?"

"Although membership in the Esoteric School has increased," the Chairman continues, "we don't seem to be able to break through a certain barrier as far as membership in the Society is concerned. In 1924 you expected to have 50,000 members in a few years. Well, many years have passed and that figure has been reached, but no more. Thousands, perhaps hundreds of thousands, take advantage of your ideas for their own selfish purposes, but don't join the Society. I must confess that it puzzles me. This rejection ..." He passes his hand over his face and wipes the sweat from his brow with a violet handkerchief. "It takes a lot of money to run this organization, as you well know. So, the more members we have who pay their dues, the better.

"But all that's only anecdotal. As you can see, everything is under control, and we don't want you around stirring things up and confusing the members. No one is ready yet for your path of knowledge, for your higher worlds and your freedom. We're still working on what you said before without having to digest new revelations. People don't really want freedom if they have to work at it themselves and you never offered to hand it to them on a silver platter. They don't even understand it — at least I don't, and who is in a better position to do so? I know by heart almost every word you ever said. In fact, I'm very fond of quoting you, as we all are, and the effect is grand. You should feel flattered."

He lights a cigarette and offers her one. She shakes her head.

"They say you used snuff then — so human." His crooked, ironic smile appears again, then vanishes.

"You see, we give them the illusion of freedom and spiritual experience through membership in the Esoteric School and the Class Readings. Why, it's better than going to church. We know what's good for them better than you ever did. The illusion makes them happy, and it gives them a sense of belonging."

She is looking at him fixedly now and he lowers his eyes. "I wish I knew what you are thinking. No, I don't care what you are thinking, if anything. You gave up on the Social Threefolding thing yourself. You fold it once, you fold it twice ... But there it is in your Complete Works, so we can't ignore it altogether. Every once in a while, someone gives a lecture about it, and young people who read about it for the first time often get enthusiastic. But we make sure that they don't go too far and offend some politician, industrialist or group of powerful members. The whole idea of a Tripartite Society is downright dangerous — for *our* Society and for the world. It implies that people are intelligent, courageous and willing to be free, which is, as I already explained, an erroneous assumption. Furthermore, what would happen to our donations if we went shooting off our mouths against political cowardice, injustice, capitalism, materialism, economic power? We talk a lot about what you said a hundred years ago, which doesn't hurt anyone's feelings now because it's so historical."

The Chairman extinguishes his cigarette in a kidney-shaped, oak ashtray, and coughs.

"And we can always counter criticism by warming up the conspiracy theory, which you so kindly bequeathed to us. You remember, don't you? The map dividing Europe? Whenever something goes wrong, we blame the Anglo-American secret societies." He smiles and looks almost happy. "It always works. Nobody's ever seen one of the secret societies, but they swallow it anyway. It's a good thing they do, for otherwise this freedom thing you were always talking about could get out of hand. It even went so far that the editors of the Society's weekly publication, which you inaugurated yourself, recently began raving about freedom of the press after insulting our best-paying members. Don't you see how dangerous that is? We kicked them out of course, and there was quite a scandal about it. 'Templegate' some wise-guy journalist called it. But it will blow over, these things always do. You should be grateful to us, but I see that you are not. That is further evidence that we know what's best for the movement and you don't. We're in the Twenty-first century, for God's sake. Cyberspace and all that. But no, you probably never even heard of it."

They sit in silence for a few moments like a couple who have been married for too long and have grown bored with each other.

"I have some ideas though," the Chairman finally says, and lights another cigarette. "I'd like to hear your opinion about them." He blows a smoke-ring over her head, which settles for a moment like a halo. It startles the Chairman, but as soon as it disappears, he forgets it. "I'm thinking of declaring myself — I mean the Chairman, whoever he is — I'm thinking of declaring the Chairman infallible, but only where thinking, feeling or willing are concerned, of course." He smiles. The woman sighs and looks out the window again.

"I think that would have an excellent effect on Society discipline. But do you know what we really need? Something that would put the icing on the cake? No? Well, I'll tell you: an immaculate conception. Problem is that our female Section Leaders are kind of old for that." He taps the desk with his long fingernails and muses: "Perhaps an Eurythmist." Suddenly his eyes light up as they do when a brainstorm strikes. "Or maybe even ..." The light goes out. "No, no, you wouldn't be interested. Well, we'll see. Miracles do happen, you know."

The conversation is becoming too one-sided, even for the Chairman, who is used to one-sided discussions, so he comes to the point.

"Now, to demonstrate my magnanimity, I am going to make you an offer."

She smiles for the first time.

"I don't know what that Mona Lisa smile is supposed to mean, and I don't care. I'm an esoteric administrator, not a psychiatrist. Here's my offer. Take it or leave it: In return for your cooperation, we will appoint you Class Reader in ... Where is it you come from now? Austria again? or is it South America? They say you were raving about the poor in Brazil or Africa or someplace."

He waits, thinking she might say something to that after all, it being so outrageous. She remains silent.

"You can be an Official Class Reader, but only on the condition that nothing is added to what you said before and is already in print. You read, you don't comment. Get it?"

"Well, what do you say?"

She shakes her head sadly.

"That's what I thought. It's just as well."

He picks up his violet telephone and asks his secretary to connect him with the *Fremdenpolizei*. His interlocutor is on the line almost immediately.

"There's a foreigner here stirring up trouble. He ... er ... no, she was arrested but I wanted to be merciful and help her. Unfortunately, I must admit that I was mistaken! She's a troublemaker and probably in the country illegally ... No, I don't know where she's from, probably somewhere in the Fourth World ... No, no, that was only a joke, don't worry. What's important is that she expresses undemocratic, un-Swiss ideas and is working without a permit. ... Yes, I will attest to it. Please come immediately and expel her — if you must, and I assume you must — from the country ... Where to? How should I know? As far away as possible, to Jupiter for all I care. But quickly, before the Summer Conference begins and we're swamped by naive people who would be dangerously susceptible to her charms."

He hangs up and looks at the woman almost, but not quite, kindly. "Believe me, it's best this way. I know what I'm doing. Your message is too important to be endangered by inflammatory preaching. We can protect the movement and the Society — which are One now, in case you've forgotten — and you can't. If we allowed you to go through with what you intend, whatever it may be, the whole thing would collapse, and we'd have to start over again."

He stands up. "You can wait in the antechamber. The *Fremdenpolizei* will be there in a moment." He looks at his watch. "In fact, they are probably there already. The Swiss are incredibly efficient when it comes to expelling foreigners. I wish you a good trip, to wherever they send you."

She stands, looks at him for the last time and turns to go.

"Wait," the Chairman says. "Tell me, why did you not name a successor?"

"You have said it," she answers, and walks through the hand-carved, arched, doorway into the antechamber where the Immigration Police are waiting. One holds handcuffs, the other a one-way ticket to Jupiter.

Shirley Locke-Holmes is the great Victorian detective's great-niece, an author greatly influenced by the great Fyodor Dostoyevsky. She is not related to the editor of this book, who is just as scandalized by its contents as you are.

by Roberto Fox

Online Activities

What is Anthroposophy?

Rudolf Steiner referred to his spiritual philosophy as 'anthroposophy,' and he defined it as 'the consciousness of one's humanity.' He was a highly trained clairvoyant who spoke from his direct cognition of the spiritual world. However, he did not see his work as a religion or as sectarian but rather sought to found a universal 'science of the spirit.' Steiner chose the term anthroposophy (from the Greek, anthropo-, human, and -sophy, wisdom) to emphasize his philosophy's humanistic orientation.

Visit the author's Southern Cross Review **e.Zine**
Visit the Rudolf Steiner e.Lib.

by Roberto Fox

www.ingramcontent.com/pod-product-compliance
Lightning Source LLC
Chambersburg PA
CBHW032048240626
47154CB00003B/1136